BONE

QUEST FOR THE SPARK
BOOK ONE

WRITTEN BY TOM SNIEGOSKI
ILLUSTRATED BY JEFF SMITH
COLOR BY STEVE HAMAKER

graphix

An Imprint of

📖SCHOLASTIC

New York   Toronto   London   Auckland   Sydney   Mexico City   New Delhi   Hong Kong

For Mulder, chasing rabbits in the Valley.
I miss you, pal.

All rights reserved. Published by Graphix, an imprint of Scholastic Inc.,
Publishers since 1920. SCHOLASTIC, GRAPHIX, and associated logos
are trademarks and/or registered trademarks of Scholastic Inc.

Library of Congress Cataloging-in-Publication Data

Sniegoski, Tom.
Quest for the spark. bk. 1 / written by Tom Sniegoski ; illustrated by Jeff Smith ;
color by Steve Hamaker. – 1st ed.
p. cm. – (Bone)
Summary: Twelve-year-old Tom Elm, his raccoon friend Roderick, Percival,
Abbey, and Barclay Bone, warrior priest Randolf, and forest woman Lorimar
join in a quest to find the pieces of the Spark that can save the Dreaming — and
the Waking World — from a Darkness created by the Nacht.
ISBN 978-0-545-14101-7
ISBN 978-0-545-14102-4 (paperback)
[1. Adventure and adventurers – Fiction. 2. Heroes – Fiction. 3. Dreams –
Fiction. 4. Magic – Fiction. 5. Fantasy. 6. Humorous stories.] I. Smith, Jeff,
ill. II. Hamaker, Steve. III. Title.
PZ7.7.S643Que 2011
[Fic] – dc22
2010017002

ACKNOWLEDGMENTS
Cover and interior artwork by Jeff Smith
Text by Tom Sniegoski
Color by Steve Hamaker

10 9 8 7 6 5 4   12 13 14

First edition, February 2011
Edited by Cassandra Pelham
Book design by Phil Falco
Creative Director: David Saylor

Printed in Singapore   46

With great love to my wife, LeeAnne, and to our newest edition, Kirby, for continuing to put up with my business.

Thanks are also due to my bestest buddy, Christopher Golden, Liesa Abrams, James Mignogna, Dave "Knives Are Quiet" Kraus, Mom and Dad Sniegoski, Mom and Dad Fogg, Pete Donaldson, and Timothy Cole and the Cult of Kali down at Cole's Comics in Lynn.

And a very special thanks to Jeff and Vijaya for trusting me with their world.

The Quest begins,
Tom

PROLOGUE

A weakened sun dawned feebly in the eastern sky, its golden rays trapped by ominous gray clouds. There wasn't the slightest chance of sunlight reaching and warming the Kingdom of Atheia far below.

Gran'ma Ben awoke with a start, that terrible gitchy feeling that made her head swim and her legs wobble rousing her from a restless sleep. This wasn't good — not good at all.

She'd had this feeling off and on for most of her life, the first time when she was just a little girl and Princess of Atheia. She later became Queen, but then she gave up the crown to move to the Valley and raise her grand-daughter, Thorn.

There's nothing worse than starting a day off with the gitchy feeling, she thought, throwing back the covers and pulling on her robe against the chill that filled her bedroom. It was an omen of bad things to come. She could spend the whole day just waiting for something to happen, and it always did. The gitchy feeling was never wrong.

And this time, Gran'ma didn't have long to wait.

She stood in front of the window in the royal castle, the damp wind tousling her white hair, and took note of the heavy sky. That was when she heard the scream, high pitched and filled with fear.

Gran'ma Ben tore from her room out into the castle hallway, eyes squinting through the early morning dimness as she searched for the source of such a horrible sound. The scream came again, and she found herself growing afraid as she ran toward it, for the scream was coming from the royal bedchamber.

From Queen Thorn's room.

Not bothering to knock, Gran'ma Ben threw open the door and charged inside. The Queen's handmaiden, Prissy, stood beside the large bed, her eyes wide and swollen with terror.

Queen Thorn lay in the center of the grand mattress, the sheets and blankets rumpled at her feet.

"What is it, Pris?" Gran'ma asked.

"I heard her cry out," Prissy said, her voice trembling. "I thought she was having a nightmare."

Queen Thorn, held firmly in the grip of sleep, moaned as her head thrashed from side to side upon her pillow.

"Looks like she still is," Gran'ma Ben said. She reached down to gently grab hold of her granddaughter's foot. Her toes were cold, like pieces of ice.

"Thorn, honey, wake up." She gave the girl's foot a shake. "It's all right, you're having a bad dream. . . . Time to wake up." The Queen moaned all the louder, whimpering pathetically.

"Thorn?" Gran'ma called again, raising her voice. She squeezed the girl's toes enough to hurt.

But still the Queen remained asleep.

"Do you see?" Prissy asked in a frightened whisper. "I tried to wake her, too . . . but she won't wake up."

Queen Thorn groaned and began to tremble with what could have been the cold, or something worse.

This was the kind of thing that Gran'ma Ben had always been afraid of, the kind of thing that she had hoped to protect her grandchild from when she'd whisked her away to hide in the Valley. But fate had a way of tracking you — like a bloodhound on a scent — and it found them, disrupting the peace that they'd had for so long.

Gran'ma reached down to the foot of the bed and pulled the covers up and over the sleeping Thorn, just as her own head began to swim and her legs began to wobble again.

It was an omen of bad things to come.

And the gitchy feeling was never wrong.

CHAPTER 1

In the early morning hours, just before dawn came to the Valley, Tom Elm was dreaming. But it wasn't the good kind of dream. It was a nightmare, and no matter how hard the twelve-year-old tried, he couldn't wake himself up.

He was drowning. Not in a lake or a pond or a rushing stream, but in a pool of blackness. He kicked his legs and splashed with his arms, fighting to keep his head above the bottomless depths. He tried to cry out for help, but every time he opened his mouth the darkness rushed in, choking him with the awful-tasting stuff of shadows.

"Help!" Tom managed, before he began to slip beneath the inky waves. *"Help me!"*

He could fight no more. Exhausted, he sank beneath the darkness, the sound of someone — *or something* — laughing in his ears. As he dropped deeper and deeper, he blindly reached out, desperate to find anything to halt his descent.

His hands brushed against something hard. It was the lucky stone that hung on a leather cord around his neck, the stone that he'd found in the oddest of places. It began to glow, softly at first, but then grew in brightness, chasing away the gloom.

Pushing back the darkness.

Tom awoke with a jolt. He could still hear the sound of liquid shadow splashing and wondered if the nightmare hadn't ended, if it had somehow followed him into the waking world.

Sitting up in bed, he saw Roderick the raccoon squatting upon a small, wooden table across the room, washing a partially eaten apple in the bowl of water that Tom's mother had left for Tom to wash his face.

"Morning, Tom," the raccoon said, shaking the water from his snack. "Did you have a bad dream?"

Tom glanced quickly at the stone still hanging around his neck. He breathed a sigh of relief when he saw it wasn't glowing anymore.

"Yeah, I think I did," he said as he threw his legs over the side of the bed and stretched. "But I'm okay now."

Roderick had been Tom's best friend since the animal came down out of the mountains over three years ago with a nasty bellyache. He'd eaten something that hadn't agreed with him and was too sick to continue his journey. Tom and

his mother had nursed the little raccoon back to health, but instead of going back up into the mountains, he'd decided to stick around. An orphan — his parents were eaten by Rat Creatures when he was just a baby raccoon — Roderick was welcomed into the Elm household. He was often treated like the brother that Tom never had, even though he did have some nasty, raccoon habits, like eating stuff that he shouldn't.

"What are you doing?" Tom asked him.

"I'm just washing my apple," Roderick said, scrubbing the piece of fruit. Raccoons were super picky about their food being clean, probably because a good part of it came from the most unappetizing places.

"But you've already eaten half of it; why wash it now?" Tom asked as he slipped into his simple tunic. "Did you find that in the garbage?" he added suspiciously, cinching the thick leather belt around his waist.

"One person's trash is another's delicious snack," Roderick stated haughtily, giving what remained of the red skin a good polish and admiring his reflection there. "Want some?" he offered.

"Think I'll wait for lunch," Tom replied, wrinkling his nose in distaste. He pulled on his short leather boots and hat. "Has my family left for the fields yet?" the boy asked, going to the bedroom door.

The raccoon nodded and jumped down from the

table, the half-eaten apple tucked beneath his furry arm. "Ages ago."

Tom moved through the empty cottage to the back door. "Why didn't they wake me up?" he asked, heading outside.

"They tried, but you were in a really deep sleep," the raccoon answered as he walked quickly beside Tom.

Tom felt a chill as flashes of his nightmare ran through his mind.

"I told them I'd get you up," Roderick said.

"And?" Tom asked.

"And then I found my beautiful apple." The raccoon stared lovingly at the partially consumed piece of fruit.

"Found it in the garbage," Tom reminded him with a laugh as he started down a winding path behind his family's house.

"It wasn't in the garbage . . . yet," the raccoon explained, struggling to keep up. "Look at it; it's still good."

Roderick tried to show him, but Tom wasn't interested. He had to get to the fields. As his father always said, the turnips weren't going to harvest themselves.

The Elm family had been turnip farmers for generations. Tom's grandfather had been a turnip farmer, and his grandfather's father had been one also. It was pretty much a given that Tom would be a turnip farmer, too, whether he wanted to be or not. The Elms were known throughout the Valley for their turnips, and this was a tradition that Tom was expected to continue.

"A little slow today, son?" Tom's father asked as he loaded a basket of turnips onto the back of a cart.

Tom hunched over and pulled a turnip out of the ground by its leafy greens. He gave the dirty root vegetable a shake before handing it to Roderick, who then carried it to a basket.

"Yes, sir," Tom said as he moved over to the next batch of leaves protruding from the fertile earth. His little sister, Lottie, giggled as she helped their mother lift another basket onto the cart.

Tom still didn't feel right. The memory of his nightmare had gradually faded away, but it left him with a sickly sense of unease.

"I didn't sleep too well last night, sir," he explained to his father. "Bad dreams."

"Bad dreams?" Tom's dad removed the floppy hat he wore to protect his bald head from the sun and wiped away the sweat of hard work with a rag from his back pocket. "Maybe if you thought a little bit more about the family business, you'd have less time for bad dreams."

"Yes, sir," Tom answered, pulling another dirty turnip from the ground.

"Maybe he's got a point," the raccoon suggested nervously. Tom scowled at his furry friend. He was the only one of his family who could understand when Roderick spoke, though sometimes he wished he couldn't.

His father placed his hat back on his head. "It looks as though you've still got a ways to go before you finish your harvest," he said sternly. "So we're going to take these baskets to market."

Lottie giggled again. She loved it when Tom got into trouble.

"Yes, sir," Tom said again, trying to pick up his pace.

"Hopefully, when we get back, you'll be done. We'll bring your basket with tomorrow's crop."

Tom nodded and pulled another turnip from the ground, brushed the dirt from it, and handed it to the waiting raccoon.

His father didn't say another word. He climbed aboard the cart to sit beside Tom's mother and little sister; then he snapped the reins, and slowly the horse began to pull the cart.

"Maybe he's got a point," Tom mimicked angrily as Roderick returned to his side.

"Well" — the raccoon prepared to defend himself — "you're always thinking that crazy stuff about being one of the Queen's soldiers."

"And what's so crazy about that?" the boy asked.

"You're a turnip farmer," Roderick said, grabbing hold of some leaves and giving them a good yank. A ripe turnip popped from the earth. "You're not a soldier."

"But I could be," Tom said. The boy stretched his spine. Harvesting turnips was murder on the back. "One of these days, I'm going to go to the Kingdom and I'm going to offer my services to Queen Thorn."

Roderick carried the turnip to the basket. "But what about the Elm family business?"

Tom shrugged. "Lottie can have it."

"That's not what your father wants," Roderick reminded him as he pulled up another turnip.

"Yeah, so what about what *I* want?" the boy asked. "What if I don't want to be a stupid turnip farmer?"

"Turnip farming isn't stupid," Roderick said.

"No, it *is* stupid . . . and it's boring!"

Roderick shook his furry head. "Turnip farming boring? No way! Remember when we found that giant turnip last season? Was that boring?"

Tom's hand immediately went to the dark stone hanging around his neck. He and Roderick had been working in the fields when Tom unearthed one of the biggest turnips either of them had ever seen. It was huge, bigger than his friend Omar's head . . . and Omar's head was pretty big.

But the vegetable was defective, its white skin marred by a jagged crack that ran the length of its round body. And inside the crack, Tom had found his rock. It had to be lucky if it was at the center of such a huge turnip. So he'd tied it to a leather thong and now wore the stone around his neck.

But really, it hadn't brought him that much luck at all.

An image suddenly flashed through Tom's mind, an image of the stone glowing like a piece of the sun and driving back the darkness that threatened to drown him.

"What's wrong?" Roderick asked. "You look like you're going to throw up."

"No," the boy answered, suddenly feeling afraid. "I . . . I just remembered something."

"Something bad?" the raccoon asked, his squeaky voice now a squeaky whisper.

"Something . . . scary," Tom replied with a gulp.

The shadows from the forest seemed to grow thicker, and Tom could have sworn they were slowly moving toward Roderick and him.

The friends finished their harvesting quickly — even Tom's father would have been impressed by their speed. Tom hefted the basket, and the two left the fields, walking side by side. Nervously, Roderick asked Tom what was wrong, but Tom didn't want to talk about his nightmare, nor did he want to talk about the shadows. He just wanted to get back to the safety of his home.

They hurried away, rushing down the winding path that would bring them back to the cottage — not seeing what was happening behind them.

They didn't see how, from the edges of the woodland that surrounded the Elm turnip fields, something began to take shape. Something made from the thick, rich dirt, the roots, rocks, vines, grass, and leaves.

A woman.

And she watched the young boy and his companion with dark, interested eyes.

CHAPTER 2

Percival F. Bone tilted his head back and, with his large, bulbous nose, sniffed the breeze coming through the open window. His nostrils twitched and flared as he tried to determine what it was he smelled. It was a talent passed down from generations of Bone adventurers and explorers, and nobody was better at it than Percival.

He could smell it in the wind, as distinct as freshly baked bread or newly mown grass. Bad weather was on the way.

"Not good," the Bone grumbled, as he gathered up the sky maps spread out atop his desk. "Not good at all." He moved toward the hallway, the navigation charts wedged beneath his arm.

"Abbey! Barclay!" he cried as he started down the winding staircase of the old family house. His niece came flying around the corner, his nephew nipping at her heels.

"What is it, Uncle Percy?" Abbey Bone asked breathlessly. She was dressed in her nicest party dress, with a bright red bow in her curly, blond, shoulder-length hair.

"Need us to do something for you, Uncle Percy?" Barclay Bone asked eagerly. He was dressed up as well, in a sport coat and bow tie.

For a minute, Percival hadn't a clue as to why the children were dressed so fancy, but then he remembered with a painful twinge of guilt. He hated to disappoint them, but today he didn't have a choice.

"Hey, I ask the questions around here," Abbey barked, jabbing an elbow into her twin brother's side. "The oldest always gets to ask the questions."

Abbey Bone was born a whole two minutes and twenty-three seconds before her brother, and she took every opportunity to remind him of it.

Barclay winced, rubbing his side.

"Need us to do something for you, Uncle Percy?" Abbey repeated, as her brother sneered.

"There's a storm coming and it smells like it's going to be a whopper," the older Bone said as he reached the bottom of the stairs. "I need you two to help me pack up the *Queen*. Looks like I'm going to have to leave early."

He could see the disappointment immediately appear on their faces.

"But what about our special night?" Abbey asked, her voice cracking.

"Yeah, we were gonna have bratwurst and sponge cake and you were gonna tell us stories about how you're this close" — Barclay Bone held up his thumb and index finger, squinting as they almost touched — "to making the greatest discovery ever in the history of Boneville."

Percival felt bad. The twins loved to have him home, and it had been less than two weeks since he'd returned from his exploration of the Jungles of Zoot. But he really did believe he was close to a historic discovery. What it was exactly, he hadn't shared with the twins, but he did know that if his newest research was correct, he was about to find something that would make him the envy of all the members of the Boneville Explorers' Society.

He could feel it in his bones, so to speak.

And now, he had to go right away or risk having his discovery uncovered by some other eager adventurer.

"Sorry, kids," Percival said as they walked down the long corridor that connected the house to his workshop and the hangar for the *Queen of the Sky*. "But discoveries like this can't wait."

"But you were gonna tell us stories about our parents, and how you taught them everything they knew about being globe-trotting adventurers," Abbey said with a sad sniffle.

Percival stopped and squatted down to speak to the little Bones.

"I know I promised, but sometimes promises have to be broken."

"Like in the pursuit of fame and fortune?" Abbey asked.

"Exactly," Percival answered. "Believe you me, there's nothing I'd rather do than have a few bratwursts and a nice slice of sponge cake with my favorite niece and nephew, but —"

"The call of adventure is screaming your name," both kids cried in unison.

"Exactly!" Percival Bone exclaimed, finger thrust into the air as he continued down the corridor toward the hangar. "Now let's use the time we have left to load up the *Queen of the Sky* with supplies and —"

He suddenly realized that he was alone.

"Where'd ya go?" he asked, turning around.

The twins still stood exactly where he'd left them, side by side, without hitting each other, a rare occurrence indeed.

"What gives?" he asked, walking back to them.

"Abbey doesn't want you to go," Barclay said.

His sister punched him savagely in the arm. "You don't want him to go either," she said.

Barclay winced, clutching his injured limb. "You're the oldest, so you don't want him to leave the most."

Percival rolled his eyes. They'd been doing this every

time he had to leave since he'd become their guardian.

"I'll be fine," he reassured them. "And if you're good while I'm gone, maybe I'll even name one of the new animals I discover after you."

"A Barclaysaurus!" the little boy suggested, his eyes twinkling with possibilities.

"Maybe," Percival teased.

"Mom and Dad said they would be fine, too," Abbey said, looking sadly at her feet.

Percival suddenly felt ashamed. He had told the twins he was going off to explore the icy regions of the Northern Territories, but in reality, he was about to embark on an expedition very much like the one that had claimed their parents — although their exact fates were still unknown.

"I promise I'll be extra careful," Percival said, crossing his heart to seal the deal. "Do you believe me?"

Abbey slowly raised her eyes to his.

"I believe you," Barclay shouted happily. His sister punched his arm again. "Oww!" he cried, gripping his now totally useless appendage. "What'd you do that for?"

Abbey's eyes were still on Percival, and he could feel a tingly sweat start to break out upon his brow.

"Why is your eye twitching, Uncle Percival?" she asked suspiciously.

Percival tried to keep his cool. "Eye twitching?" He laughed nervously. "My eye isn't twitching . . . it's just a little itchy from all the dust in this old house." He started to cough and rubbed at his eyes. "It's just my allergies."

Abbey placed her hands upon her tiny hips and studied him carefully. "It's kinda funny," she said. "Mom and Dad always said that they could tell when you was lying because your right eye twitched."

"Lying? Me? Don't be silly," Percival said indignantly. He unsnapped the button on one of the many pockets of his safari shirt, removed a handkerchief, and quickly dabbed at the nervous sweat on his brow.

"I'll have to call Mrs. Doozle and ask her to stay with you while I'm gone. Maybe she'll bring that trained ocelot of hers and . . ." He tried to change the subject as he stuffed the damp cloth back into his pocket.

"You're lying about something." Abbey stamped her foot.

Percival gasped and covered up his now wildly twitching right eye. "I am not," he proclaimed weakly.

"Now you're lying about lying!" Abbey announced.

Percival was speechless, trapped by his niece's accusations.

"Stop it, Abbey," Barclay ordered. "What are you thinking? Uncle Percy would never lie to us." The little boy looked to his uncle for backup. "Right, Unc? You would never do such a thing."

Percival was about to lie again but couldn't stand the way Abbey was looking at him anymore. He had no choice but to come clean with the youngsters.

"I'm afraid your sister's right," he announced with a heavy sigh and a shake of his head. "But I want you to understand that I did it for your own good."

"Why, Uncle Percy?" Barclay asked. "What's so bad that you couldn't tell us the truth?"

"It's about where you're really going on your next adventure, isn't it?" Abbey asked with a seriousness not befitting a child her age. Percival suddenly realized he should have been locking his study door. Someone had been peeking at his research.

"I didn't want you guys to be afraid," he explained.

"Where are you going?" Barclay asked.

"He's going to try and find the Valley," Abbey said bitterly, her eyes brimming with tears. "He's gonna try to find the Valley and never come back, just like Mom and Dad."

Percival bent down and swept the twins into his arms. "No, no. That's not it, not it at all." He held them tightly, hoping they could feel how much they meant to him . . . how much he loved them.

"My plan is to find the Valley, *and* what happened to your parents, and come back to you as quick as I can."

"But the Boneville Explorers' Society says that the

Valley doesn't even exist, and that Mom and Dad probably got lost and died in the uncharted territories," Abbey said, her little voice choked with emotion.

"But we don't believe that, do we, Uncle Percival?" Barclay chimed in, his big, brown eyes filled with wonder.

Just like his father's, Percival thought. "No, we don't," he replied.

"We don't believe them because the Bone cousins went to the Valley, didn't they, Uncle Percival?"

"I believe they did."

Abbey pulled away from her uncle's embrace and crossed her arms angrily. "The Boneville Explorers' Society says that the Bone cousins are big fat liars."

"The Boneville Explorers' Society says a lot of things that I don't agree with," Percival told her.

"I don't agree with them either," Barclay added.

Abbey scowled. "Well, you should," she snapped. "'Cause if Mom and Dad had listened to them, they'd still be with us now." She looked as though she was about to cry, so Percival reached out to console her. But Abbey stepped back, avoiding his attempt.

Percival accepted her anger and ran a hand across his lower jaw as he tried to figure out how to best explain himself. "Your mom and dad were two of the bravest explorers I ever knew. They believed the Valley was out there, and they were determined to do everything in their power to find it, in spite of what the Boneville Explorers' Society said. . . . That's just the way they were." He placed a hand on his chest as he looked at his niece. "Sorry to say, I'm that way, too."

"Me, too!" Barclay proclaimed, puffing out his chest proudly.

Abbey pulled back her fist, but the boy jumped away before her blow could fall.

"I never wanted to hurt you guys," Percival said. "I just didn't want you to worry."

"Like that's not gonna happen," Abbey said, rolling her eyes.

"What if I promise to be extra-extra careful," Percival said. "And come back as soon as I can."

"And no side trips?" Abbey asked.

He shook his head. "No side trips."

The explorer waited for the little girl's response, as did her brother.

"Well?" Barclay nudged. "What's it gonna be . . . do you believe him or not?"

She was very serious, scrutinizing Percival with a stare so intense he could practically hear the gears turning inside her little head. But then her expression softened, and Abbey rewarded his honesty with a smile.

"I believe you." She rushed to throw her arms around his waist. "But please come back soon, 'cause you wouldn't want to make a habit out of lying to little kids."

"That would be a most horrible thing," Percival agreed, returning the child's hug.

Barclay approached for a share of his uncle's affection, but Abbey lashed out, punching him in the shoulder. The boy bellowed.

"That's for trying to rush me," she snarled. "Never rush the oldest."

Uncle Percival straightened up. "All right, you two, enough horsing around," he said. "We've got a lot of work to do if I want to be in the sky before the storm hits."

"Not sure how much good I'm gonna be, Unc," the boy said. "That last punch made my arm all rubbery." Barclay flopped his arm as if it suddenly had no bones.

"Work it out, boy!" the older Bone said. "You're going to need both arms if you're going to help me load up the *Queen*."

Percival practically ran down the rest of the corridor to the heavy wooden door at the end. He reached into his pocket and removed a large, old-fashioned key, stuck it into the lock, and turned it.

"Time is of the essence." He swung the door open to reveal his most prized possession.

The *Queen of the Sky*.

Percival strode into the large, glass-ceilinged room that housed the *Queen of the Sky.* At one time, the room had been a greenhouse responsible for some of the most lovely and colorful flowers grown in Boneville, but not since Percival had taken over the old home. Now it was his workshop and the resting place for his amazing sky ship. Percival got a special kind of thrill every time he saw her — there was nothing more beautiful.

The *Queen*'s body was made of the strongest and most durable wood from the forests of Boneville. It resembled a sailing ship, but instead of sails, it had three large balloons to carry it, balloons that were currently being filled with hot gas in preparation for his voyage. Powerful propellers on either side of the craft gave it thrust and direction. There wasn't anyplace that the *Queen of the Sky* couldn't go.

Percival glanced up through the glass ceiling at the angry sky outside. The storm was coming much faster than he had anticipated, and by its smell, it was going to be worse than he had thought.

He headed straight for the supplies and special equipment that were stacked in front of the vessel. Abbey and Barclay were already eagerly carrying boxes up the gangplank and into the ship.

"How're we doing, kids?" Percival asked as he picked up two boxes and followed them up the plank.

"You sure have a lot of boxes of potatoes here, Unc,"

Barclay said. "How long are you planning to be gone again?"

Percival laughed. "One can never have too many potatoes, son," he said. "Especially when they're the main power source for your sky ship."

Percival F. Bone was a regular pioneer when it came to the use of new and unusual scientific discoveries. He was the only — as far as he knew — explorer in all of Boneville who was currently using the untapped potential of the potato as a power source. Inside the starchy, vegetable tuber was electrical energy just waiting to be used, and he was more than happy to oblige.

Abbey stood aboard the *Queen*, looking up through the glass ceiling at the ominous gray clouds billowing above the Bone ancestral home.

"Are you sure you want to be going up in that, Uncle Percy?" Abbey asked when the winds outside began to moan.

"It'll be fine," Percival said, taking more boxes from his nephew as the boy reached the top of the gangplank. "My nose tells me the storm won't be here for at least another hour."

Percival was heading down to retrieve some more supplies when the hangar grew very, very dark, and a sound much like that of a runaway steam locomotive filled the

air. He glanced up and saw that it had become as black as night outside, and the wind had formed a funnel that was sucking up everything from rocks to trees.

"Hey, Uncle Percy?" Abbey called from the deck of the *Queen*. "Has your nose ever been wrong?"

"Oh, once or twice," the older Bone answered just as the storm roared like some huge, prehistoric beast and crashed through the roof.

The storm was a monster.

A swirling cone of howling wind and dirt ferociously shattered the glass ceiling. It dropped down through the open skylight into the converted greenhouse, searching for new prey to consume.

Percival watched in horror as the angry twister began to tear apart everything in its path. It had taken several years to convert the old greenhouse into his workshop, but the storm was making short work of it in no time flat. The spinning funnel ripped up the floorboards and gobbled down the wood, still hungry for more as it traveled through the room.

Years of adventuring had taught Percival to act quickly and calmly to avoid calamity, which was exactly what was unfolding before him now.

Barclay stood frozen, watching as the swirling, debris-filled body of the tornado slowly made its way toward him, sucking up everything in its wake.

His nephew would be next if Percival didn't shake a leg. He leaped from the gangplank to the floor, screaming the boy's name, hoping to break the hypnotic spell that the violent wind had over the child. At first he didn't think the boy had heard him above the roar of the tornado's rampage, but then Barclay turned his head toward his uncle.

"Uncle Percy!" he shrieked fearfully.

Behind him, the ravenous storm was picking up boxes and crates of potatoes and replacement parts for the *Queen*'s engines, voraciously filling its spinning belly. It seemed like Percival would be too late, but as long as there was even the slightest chance he could reach his nephew, Percival F. Bone, adventurer extraordinaire, had to risk it. And that's what he did as he flung himself at the boy, picked him up, and threw him over his shoulder. Then he quickly turned around and raced back to the *Queen*, the storm chomping at his heels.

"Run, Uncle Percy, run!" Barclay yelled.

Percival could feel the storm's cold, damp breath upon his neck, the rumble of its pursuit vibrating what remained of the floor beneath his pounding feet. He bounded up the gangplank toward the deck of the *Queen of the Sky*, where Abbey waited for them, panic on her young face.

"Hurry!" she screamed over the howl of the rabid storm. "It's right behind you!"

Percival was only a few feet away from the *Queen* when he felt the gangplank begin to move like a chew toy being shaken by a dog. He tensed the muscles in his legs and sprang for the deck . . . just as the plank was yanked from beneath him by the raging twister.

Barclay screamed like the dickens in Percival's ear as they soared through the tumultuous air — and began to drop like stones mere inches from the side of the *Queen*. A quick-thinking Abbey grabbed a rope from the deck and tossed it over the side. Percival's hands shot out like lightning and took hold of the rope. He hauled himself and his dangling passenger up the side of the sky ship as the storm winds picked at them.

"Nice one," Percival exclaimed as Abbey helped them over the rail and onto the deck.

"I thought you two were goners," she said, and hugged them both tightly.

"And we might still be," Percival said, as the *Queen of the Sky* began to pitch and roll and then to spin madly around. The storm snapped the thick ropes that moored the sky craft to the greenhouse floor as if they were made of thread, and pulled the *Queen of the Sky* into its whirling body. It swallowed the ship, and all who were on board, in one voracious gulp.

CHAPTER 3

Randolf Clearmeadow's pain never went away, but that was something he had grown used to over the long years. Almost everyone in the small village of Trumble and in the dingy tavern where he spent most of his time knew of his past, and of his shame. The hurtful memories came as they always did, and Randolf knew that he would need more mugs of ale to push them away, and for that he would have to spin tales of the past — when he was of the Veni Yan.

When he was a hero.

He checked the four mugs stacked in front of him, just to be sure they were empty, and sadly they were. Pushing back his chair, the former warrior priest left the dark corner and slowly shuffled to the center of the room. He searched the crowd for someone he did not recognize, anyone to hear his stories and supply his drink.

"May I interest you in a story of the past, good traveler?" he asked a man who casually puffed upon a pipe, smoke billowing from the corner of his mouth.

"And what would this tale cost me?" the man asked, his flagon of ale before him.

Randolf stared at the man's refreshment, wishing that it was his. "A drink," he said. "A drink to help me remember the glories of days past, and to forget sorrows too heavy to bear."

The man continued to puff upon his pipe, then finally reached into a leather purse that hung from his belt. He removed a single coin and, after a slight pause, placed it on the table and slid it toward Randolf.

"Will this be enough?" he asked.

It was more than enough, and the former Veni Yan's mouth began to water in anticipation. He reached for the coin, but the man was faster, and his hand quickly covered it.

"It had better be a good story," he said. "Something exciting." He lifted his hand to expose the coin again.

Randolf grabbed it and headed for the bar.

"I want to hear about the Nights of Lightning," the man called out behind him. "Do you have a story of them?"

The Nights of Lightning.

Randolf's back stiffened at the mention of that time

when the monstrous Hairy Men came down from the mountains to lay siege to the Valley's villages and farms.

His hand shook as he grabbed his flagon from the barkeep and quickly brought it to his thirsty mouth.

Yes, he had a story, a story of how during one of those long, terrible nights, when the Veni Yan did battle against the hairy creatures, he lost everything that was dear to him.

He saw them again, his wife and daughter, as they stood solemnly in the doorway to their home, waving good-bye. They hated to see him go, afraid that each time he left would be the time he didn't return. But they were brave as always as they watched him head off to chase the Hairy Men back into the hills. Brave before they died because he wasn't there to protect them.

Yes, Randolf had a story, but it was one that he would do just about anything to forget.

"I have nothing about the Nights of Lightning," Randolf said, turning from the bar to the traveler. "Perhaps a thrilling tale of how I single-handedly defeated a band of robbers on my way to Atheia and —"

"You know something about it," the traveler said as he added more tobacco to his pipe. "When I mentioned the Nights, your whole body trembled."

Randolf drank some more.

"A bit of a chill in the air," he said. "Nothing more."

"I want my story," the traveler said with a growl. "I paid good money, and I want to hear about the Nights of Lightning."

Randolf's anger surged, and he quickly turned toward his table in the shadows. "Then you'll hear nothing," he said.

He heard the sound of a chair overturn behind him and felt a solid grip upon his arm.

"Then you owe me for the drink," the traveler said roughly. "Or should I call for the Constable?"

Randolf didn't take his eyes from his table in the corner. "I think you should remove your hand from my arm," he said calmly.

"Or what?" the man sneered. "You'll drink me to death?" His grip grew tighter on Randolf's arm. "Look at you," he said with disdain. "You're less than a shadow of what you were . . . Stick-eater."

Rage flowed through Randolf. Hearing the derogatory name for a Veni Yan warrior priest ignited a fury inside him that he didn't think he was capable of having anymore. He pulled his arm away and turned to confront the man who had dared insult him and the faith that had at one time defined his way of life.

And the strangest thing happened.

The tavern was suddenly gone, replaced by a world the likes of which he had not seen since his earliest days of study, before his mystical third eye had been blinded by sadness.

It was the Dreaming . . . and something was wrong. When he'd last glimpsed it, the Dreaming was the most peaceful land he had ever seen, a world of the utmost calm and beauty, but now . . .

A darkness had spread across the land, a physical shadow that weighed down the branches of the trees and stained the fields of gold an oily black. Thick clouds of gray, far too close to the ground, oozed across the normally tranquil skies, bringing with them a low, rumbling sound like that of a fearsome predator preparing to pounce.

A million questions ran through his mind — the first and foremost, how he came to be in this place — but they all became less than important as he watched the darkness flow toward him, spreading faster as if it knew he was standing there.

Sensing danger, Randolf slowly backed away, watching as tentacles of solid black emerged from the darkness, snaking toward him with incredible swiftness. The first of the tendrils to reach him wrapped tightly around his ankle, and a paralyzing cold spread up his leg. Another lashed around one arm, and yet another about his waist.

The former Veni Yan struggled in their grasp, trying desperately to free himself as the tentacles of darkness leeched the warmth from his body. Finally he realized there was no choice. He had to fight.

Randolf was cold. So very, very cold. A part of him wanted to do nothing, to let the living darkness take him. But still he strained to reach inside his tunic, searching for the dagger that rested there. For another part of him was not yet ready to die, and he knew that his wife and little girl would understand.

Gathering his strength, the former warrior cried out, pulling what was supposed to be his knife from its scabbard but finding that he now held something else in his hand. He was certain it was a knife, but it was made of light, and glowed like white-hot metal.

The shadows screeched in displeasure, recoiling from his mysterious new weapon. Randolf frantically cut away at the thick ropes of black that held him fast, his heart pumping wildly as he spun to face the serpents of shadow that slithered toward him. He did not shy away. He lunged at the blackness and plunged his glowing knife deep into its rubbery shadow flesh. The darkness moaned its pain as Randolf found again his warrior spirit.

"Back!" he commanded, slashing his dagger of light

across the slick, ebony surface. The darkness reared back to form a solid wave, and Randolf braced himself as it surged forward to engulf him in its oily embrace.

To drown him in shadow.

The old warrior jumped backward and crashed into a table, spilling nearly full flagons of ale. He slashed at the air, noticing that his weapon no longer glowed. And this was not the only thing that had changed. Confused, Randolf looked around. He was back in the tavern, and the place was a mess. Overturned chairs and tables were strewn about, and frightened customers huddled beside the bar.

"He's lost his head," a patron who Randolf knew as Jon Wheelbarrow whispered.

"Too much ale is what I say," Thin William said with a nod. "It's pickled his brains, it has."

"Alls I wanted was my story," the traveler whispered. "And when I asked him for what was rightfully mine, he lost his mind."

"You don't understand," Randolf began. He made a move toward the customers, and they all jumped back. "I had no idea . . . a moment ago, I was in the Dreaming. . . ."

"That's close enough, Randolf Clearmeadow," Robert the barkeep warned. "We don't want any more trouble from the likes of you."

"But . . . but I was fighting for my life," he tried to explain. Yet it was no use. The patrons looked at one another, fear in their eyes. They thought he was insane, and who knew — maybe they were right.

The former warrior stopped his advance and began to right the tables and chairs. "I'm sorry," he apologized. "I don't know what happened. . . . Let me help. . . ."

"There he is!" a voice suddenly cried.

Randolf recognized the farmer who entered the tavern as Dingus Brinbridge. The old man scowled and pointed a crooked finger at Randolph, directing a group of men who followed close behind him.

"He's a menace and should be locked up," the old farmer said, and the other patrons, still huddled by the bar, heartily agreed.

Constable Roarke was the last to enter, a large man with a curled, black mustache. His three deputies parted to let him pass as he strode into the tavern and drew his sword.

"Drop your weapon," the Constable growled at Randolf, who hadn't even realized he was still holding his knife. Quickly he opened his hand and let the blade fall to the floor with a clatter.

"I meant no harm," the former Veni Yan monk attempted, although he sensed it would do him little good, for the deputies had all drawn their swords as well.

"Take him," the Constable commanded, the hint of a cruel smile beneath the loop of his mustache.

The deputies came at Randolf as one, with violence twinkling in their eyes.

CHAPTER 4

The Rat Creature's stomach rumbled, sounding like huge boulders rolling down a hill.

"I'm so hungry," he moaned to his Rat Creature friend.

"I'm not listening," his comrade said, plugging his pointy ears with long, clawed fingers. "If I listen, you're going to get us in trouble."

"But you saw it, didn't you?"

His friend removed his fingers from his ears.

"Yes, yes, I saw it, but it doesn't matter because it does not belong to us."

"But we saw it first," the Rat Creature said, wringing his hands together nervously. "The King had no right to —"

"King Agak has every right," the Other Rat Creature interrupted, wagging a finger at his friend. "That is what makes him king."

The Rat Creature paused, playing with the tiny rib cage of one of the previous meals that littered the floor of their cave — along with many other bones of various sizes and shapes.

"That was the most delicious dead squirrel I've ever seen," he said, tears in his dark, bulbous eyes.

His comrade slapped a hand to his furry forehead in disbelief.

"But King Agak has claimed it as his own, and that is the end of this sad story," he snapped.

Ignoring his friend, the Rat Creature continued. "Just think of all the delicious ways we could have enjoyed its succulent, decomposing flesh," he said, a thick string of drool dripping from his mouth onto the fur of his chest.

"I don't want to hear it!" the Rat's friend roared.

"Squirrel stew, barbecued squirrel, squirrel fricassee . . ."

"I'm not listening!" the Other screeched louder. "LA-LALALALA!"

"Squirrel kabobs . . . squirrel quiche . . ."

The Rat Creature's companion suddenly stopped his noise and turned to look at his ravenous friend. "What did you just say?" he asked, his mouth twitching.

"Squirrel quiche."

The Other remained silent, a clawed finger thoughtfully tapping upon one of his jagged, razor-sharp teeth.

"We need that squirrel," he finally said.

The Rat Creature nodded vigorously. "I couldn't agree with you more."

They were as quiet as mice — small, succulent mice that would have popped so juicily into their mouths if there had been mice to eat, but, alas, there was only a dead squirrel, and that had been stolen from them.

The two Rat Creatures scurried down the winding stone tunnel within the cave system that they called home. The mountains were honeycombed with these caves, and the great King Agak had of course claimed the largest as his own.

"We found it fair and square," the Rat Creature complained to his friend.

"Quiet!" the Other hissed, placing a clawed finger to his wide, jack-o'-lantern mouth. "You don't want to wake him."

It was widely known that the great King Agak enjoyed his naps and could often be found snoozing the day away in the darkness of his cavern lair.

The Rat Creature immediately lowered his voice to a whisper. "Is it so wrong to take back what's rightfully ours?" he asked.

His comrade shook his shaggy head. "Not at all; we just

don't want to get caught. . . . I don't think it would be good for our health."

The Rat Creature considered this. "The King really isn't known for his compassion, is he?"

"He does have some anger issues," the Other Rat Creature agreed.

They peered through the darkness down to the end of the passage, where they knew the King was napping.

"Maybe you were right; maybe we should just look for another dead thing," the Rat Creature suggested, realizing the severity of what they were about to do.

"What, and have him take that from us as well? Never! Let's go liberate our precious, decomposing tree rodent from the clutches of our oppressor."

The Rat Creature, overwhelmed by his comrade's stirring words, began to softly clap. "Yes! Yes, we can!" he said, and without another moment's hesitation, continued to stalk the darkened tunnel to the King's quarters, his comrade following close behind.

SNORRRRRRRRRKKKKKKKK!
SNORRRRRRRRRKKKKKKKKKKK!

The sudden sound from the King's chamber was terrifying, stopping the Rat Creature dead in his tracks. His partner in crime crashed into him, and they both nearly spilled into the room.

"What's wrong?" the Other Rat Creature asked in a panicked whisper. "Why have you stopped?"

"Listen," the Rat Creature commanded. "I think there's some kind of beast inside the King's chamber."

SNORRRRRRRRRKKKKKKKK!

SNORRRRRRRRRRKKKKKKKKKK!

SNORRRRRRRRRRKKKKKKKKKKKK!

They looked at each other, terrified, on the verge of fleeing for their lives.

"Wait," the Rat Creature's comrade whispered, listening closely to the disturbing sounds.

SNORRRRRRRRRKKKKKKKK!

"I think that's the King," he suggested. "I think he's snoring."

The Rat Creature cautiously craned his neck into the chamber for a peek.

SNORRRRRRRRRKKKKKKKKK!

"You're right," he agreed. "You'd think he would have seen a doctor for that. I'm surprised the whole mountain isn't complaining."

"Never mind that. Do you see the squirrel?"

Again the Rat Creature peered around the curved, rock entry into the darkened cavern. He could see their leader lying in the center of the cave, deep in the embrace of sleep, his arms wrapped around the dead squirrel, his face resting on its decaying body as on a pillow.

"I see it all right, but I don't like what I'm seeing," the Rat Creature whispered.

The Other slunk up beside him and took a peek for himself. "Oh my," he said with concern. "This isn't going to be easy, is it?"

"What is, these days," the Rat Creature said with a sigh.

They stood in silence, listening as their leader noisily slept.

"Are we actually going to attempt this?" the Rat Creature's companion asked him.

"What choice do we have? Can you not smell the delicious aroma of decay from that corpse that belongs to us?"

"Well, when you put it that way . . ." the Other said.

SNORRRRRRRRKKKKKKK! added the King, as if daring them to act.

"So how should we proceed?" the Rat Creature asked his friend. "Should we just grab it and run?"

"Wouldn't that wake him?"

SNORRRRRRRRRKKKKKKKKKKKKK!

"Ya think?" the Rat Creature asked. "Seems like he's a pretty heavy sleeper."

"Yes, but we wouldn't want to take the chance. I think pure stealth is in order here."

"All right," the Rat Creature said. "Be stealthy." He gestured toward where the King slept. "I'll be right here."

"Oh no," his comrade corrected. "We'll do this together."

"Do tell."

"Using great skill, I will cause the King to relinquish his grip upon our prize, and it will be your job to quickly snatch it away," the Other Rat Creature explained.

The Rat Creature thought for a moment, then a large, toothy smile spread across his hairy face. "Y'know, that just might work." He gestured again for his friend to proceed, eager to have this over and done and their precious dead squirrel back in their possession.

The Other Rat Creature crouched down low and crawled on his belly across the cavern floor toward the sleeping King.

SNORRRRRRRRKKKKKKKKKKKKK!

Slowly, and oh so carefully, the Other rose up, looming over the snoring figure. The King was sprawled on his stomach, arms wrapped around the dead animal, his face nuzzling the squirrel's rotting carcass.

"Go on," the Rat Creature urged.

His comrade reached down toward the King's flaring nostrils. With the tip of one of his long claws, he gently tickled the ruler's nose. The King snorted loudly, his repulsive face contorting in discomfort, but he did not wake. Again, the Other reached down and teased the King's nose. This time the King began to squirm, one hand letting go of the squirrel to scratch at the annoyance.

"Almost," the Rat Creature hissed eagerly, his mouth watering in anticipation.

His companion reached a third time, but just as he was about to run his claw along the King's nostril, their leader surged up with a loud snort, wrapped his arms around the startled Rat, and dragged him down to the cave floor. The Other wanted to scream as the King hugged him tight, rubbing his nasty king face in the fur of his stomach as he drifted back into a deep sleep.

Trapped in the King's embrace, the Other Rat Creature looked for help from his friend but saw that his attentions were focused elsewhere. For he had seized the opportunity to retrieve their precious prize and was now holding the dead squirrel before him. The Rat Creature stared lovingly at the rotting rodent, oblivious to his comrade's predicament.

"A little help here," the Other squeaked softly as the King drew him closer. But the Rat Creature wasn't listening, mesmerized — it appeared — by the sight of the dead squirrel.

"Hello? Remember me?" the Other hissed, trying not to rouse the King. The Rat Creature didn't respond as he stared at his prize, trails of thick drool flowing from his mouth like a slimy waterfall.

And then the unthinkable happened.

With the King still snuggling him, the Other Rat Creature watched with disbelieving eyes as his friend, one he would normally have trusted with his life, began to slowly bring the dead squirrel . . . *their* dead squirrel . . . toward his open maw.

The Other Rat Creature was speechless. He was going to do it . . . his friend . . . his bosom buddy . . . was going to betray their friendship, and for what? The delicious, decaying flesh of a tree rodent? Just as his one-time BFF prepared to shove the entire body of the dead squirrel into his mouth, the Other cried out in anger, which really wasn't a very smart thing to do.

"Don't. You. Dare," he bellowed, stopping his friend cold.

And waking up the King.

The room erupted in chaos. The King's eyes snapped open, and he let out an ear-piercing scream, pushing away the Rat Creature that he'd been cuddling in his arms.

"What are you doing here?" the King shouted, his short, muscular body rising up from where he'd been lying. He wasn't as tall as Kingdok, the Rat Creatures' last king, but he was twice as scary and had four times as many teeth.

The Other Rat had to think quickly or he was most assuredly doomed. "A thousand pardons, my good King," he said with a nervous bow. "I was on patrol when I heard some suspicious noises coming from your chamber."

"Yes, suspicious noises!" the Rat Creature exclaimed from the entryway.

The King yelped and spun around, surprised to see a second Rat Creature in his royal chambers. "You were *both* on patrol?" Agak asked, squinting suspiciously.

"Oh yes," the Other answered casually. "We're always doing that."

"We're patrollers from way back," said the Rat Creature, waving his hands around — one of which contained the dead squirrel.

"I thought it might be a bear," the Other Rat Creature said quickly, trying to distract the King by moving his clawed hands about.

The King turned to him. "A bear?"

"Yes, a bear . . . a bear looking for trouble," the Other said, nodding furiously. "So we rushed in and searched the cave, just to be certain that you were safe."

From behind the King, the Rat Creature agreed with his comrade. "The place was full of bears." He tapped the squirrel against his chin in thought. "There had to be at least twenty of them in here."

"Twenty bears?" the King questioned disbelievingly.

The Other nodded furiously, trying to keep the King's attention. "He's right. There were at least twenty of the beasts in here. It's a good thing we were in the neighborhood."

"Who knows what would have happened if we hadn't stopped by," the Rat Creature said, waving the rotting rodent in the King's direction as he joined his friend's side.

"Well, our work here is done," the Other Rat Creature said quickly, before grabbing his friend's arm and pulling him toward the cave entrance. "We should be on our way and let the King get back to his beauty sleep."

They both backed into the entrance and were just about to turn and flee with their sacred prize, when the King spoke.

"Where are you going with my squirrel?"

The Rats froze. Slowly they turned to each other, their round eyes connecting.

"Run!" exclaimed the Rat Creature.

"And we were doing so well," his partner in crime said as they scrabbled to escape, their King's screams of outrage and murderous fury chasing them into the passage.

CHAPTER 5

The sun had set hours before, but Tom had yet to turn in for the night.

"What are you making?" Roderick asked from where he sat on the windowsill. The window was open and a cool breeze blew through the boy's room.

Tom sat at a small table he'd made from discarded pieces of wood that his father had used to repair their turnip cart. He was carving a thick tree branch he and Roderick had found on their way back from harvesting that afternoon.

"You'll see when I'm done," Tom said, concentrating.

"Don't you think you should be in bed?" the raccoon asked. "It's getting pretty late and you're gonna hafta get up early in the morning."

"I'm not tired." Tom took a final slice from the end of the stick and set his knife down. "Finished," he said with a smile as he admired his work.

"You made a sword?" Roderick asked. He jumped down from the window to join the boy. "Big deal, you've made tons of swords."

"This isn't just any sword," Tom said, holding it up by its carved hilt. "This sword belongs to the Captain of the Guard."

"Captain of the Guard?" Roderick asked, suddenly interested. "Who's that?"

Tom sliced the air with the wooden blade. "That's me."

"You? Don't be silly; you're just a boy."

"Yeah, right now," Tom replied. He lunged and thrust as if in the midst of battle. "But in a few years I'm gonna be Captain of the Guard and protect Queen Thorn."

"Protect her from what?"

"I don't know." Tom swung at his imaginary foes and ducked beneath their attempts to separate his head from his shoulders. "Anything she needs protecting from."

"If you're gonna be the captain, can I be one of the guards?" Roderick jumped up and down excitedly.

"Sorry." The boy shook his head. "I don't think they let raccoons be in the palace guard."

"Darn," the raccoon said, kicking at a piece of dirt on the floor.

"But you can help me defeat the evil," Tom said, bounding across the room and up onto his bed.

"All right." Roderick scampered across the floor and up the side of the bed to join his friend. "Who are we fighting?"

"A whole buncha Hairy Men," Tom said excitedly, swinging his wooden sword wildly. "Take that, you filthy Rat Creatures!" he exclaimed. Roderick suddenly jumped off the bed and returned to the windowsill.

"What's wrong, Roderick?" Tom asked, halting his imaginary battle. "Don't you want to help me defeat the Rat Creatures?"

The raccoon stared out at the night. "Naw, think I'm just gonna go to sleep," he said sadly.

And then it dawned on Tom, and he felt as stupid as could be. Roderick's family — his mother and father — had been killed by the Rat Creatures.

Tom jumped from the bed. "I'm sorry, Roderick," he said. "I wasn't thinking. . . . I forgot all about how your mom and dad were . . ."

"You don't have to be sorry," Roderick said with a sniffle. He wiped his dark eyes and forced a smile. "It's all right, I know you didn't mean nothing by it."

Tom moved closer and put his free hand on Roderick's shoulder.

"Goblins," he said.

"What about 'em?" Roderick asked, wiping his nose with the back of his paw.

"We could fight goblins. . . . How's that sound?"

"That sounds . . ."

"That sounds like a young man who needs to go to bed immediately," said a stern voice.

Tom and Roderick looked over to see Tom's mother standing in the doorway, arms crossed.

"But I'm not tired yet," Tom protested. He was actually exhausted after his long day, but the thought of going to sleep made him queasy. He didn't want a repeat of the night before; he didn't want a repeat of the bad dreams.

"And that tells me you're too tired to think straight," his mother said. She went to the bed and pulled down the covers.

"No more guff," she said. "To bed with you."

Tom sighed, dragging his wooden sword behind him as he headed for the bed. His mother ruffled his hair as he wriggled beneath the blankets.

"And give me that stick," she commanded, putting her hand out. "You'll poke your eye out."

"I'd rather not," Tom said, suddenly feeling very protective of his new weapon.

"And why not?" she asked, placing her hands on her hips.

"Because . . . because I might need it," Tom said, remembering the bad dream from that morning and thinking that maybe — *maybe* — the sword might help him keep the bad dreams away.

"It's bedtime; what could you possibly need a stick for?" his mother asked.

"It's actually the Captain of the Guard's sword," Roderick chattered to her as he climbed up onto the bed to join his friend, but Tom's mother didn't understand.

"It's special," Tom told her.

"Oh, is it?" Tom's mother asked, pulling the covers up under Tom's chin and giving him a peck on the head. "Well, don't come cryin' to me if you get yourself good and poked in the middle of the night," she warned.

"I won't," Tom promised. "I'll be careful."

She smiled, then blew out the candle. "Good night, Tom," she said.

"Good night, Mama."

"Good night, Roderick," she added from the doorway.

"Night, ma'am."

With Tom's mother gone, the two friends lay in the darkness.

"No bad dreams, Tom," Roderick whispered. "Okay?"

"No bad dreams," Tom agreed, rolling over and closing his eyes, but just in case, he clutched the special sword to his chest.

Tom didn't remember falling asleep, but he must have, for he awoke with a start in a place that he didn't recognize. He was still in his bed, warm and snug beneath the covers, but he was also in a forest — the most beautiful forest he had ever seen. Roderick was still asleep, curled in a tight little ball at the foot of the bed, snoring loudly.

"Roderick," Tom said, reaching down to give his friend a poke. "Roderick, wake up." But the raccoon remained asleep, no matter how hard Tom poked him. Nervously, Tom reached beneath the covers and withdrew his sword, holding it before him as protection against . . .

Against what, he didn't know.

The forest was incredibly dense, the trees growing closely together, their thick, dark leaves filtering out any chance of sunlight. Tom couldn't tell if it was day or night here. Cautiously, he left his bed. The grass was unusually warm beneath his bare feet, despite the damp chill in the air. The cool wind rustled the leaves of the trees around him, and the air smelled of the most fragrant flowers.

As he took everything in, Tom couldn't help but feel that he had been here before. He stood beside his bed, glancing at Roderick. "You're gonna be mad you missed this," he said to the still-snoring raccoon.

The hair on the back of his neck suddenly prickled, and Tom sensed that he was no longer alone. He looked around quickly, sword raised.

"Hello?" he called out to the trees that swayed in the breeze.

"Hello to you," a woman's voice replied.

"Where are you?" Tom asked. "Show yourself."

A lone figure, dressed in a long, hooded robe, emerged from the thick of the forest. The trees and bushes seemed to move from her path, allowing her to pass.

"I felt that you should see this," the woman said, lifting one of her arms to direct the boy's attention. "See it as it was before the awakening of the Nacht."

"Nacht?" Tom asked, the word feeling strange as it rolled off his tongue.

It suddenly became very cold, and the wind no longer carried the smell of flowers. Now something bitter and rotten hung in the air.

"What's happening?" the boy asked in alarm.

A seat of rock emerged from the earth, and the hooded figure slowly sat down upon it.

"Not what *is* . . . but what *has* happened," the woman said. "This forest isn't like it once was, and sadly, neither am I."

It was becoming darker as a thick, oily gloom, like liquid shadow, seeped down from the branches of the trees and spread across the once beautiful landscape. Tom clutched his sword tighter.

"This is what became of the Dreaming, once the Nacht was awakened," the woman said, her features still hidden by the hood of her robe.

"The Dreaming?" Tom questioned. "Then all this is . . . is just a dream?" He looked back to his bed and the sleeping Roderick. "Nothing can hurt me . . . or my friend . . . right?"

She was momentarily silent. "If only that were true," she finally answered, then reached up with a pale hand and pulled back her hood. The woman was younger than Tom expected. Her skin was a delicate white, like fine silk, and her dark eyes glistened wetly. She was strangely beautiful, but something about her told Tom that she was also very sad.

The darkness suddenly rushed at him like a flood. Tom raced toward his bed, trying to outrun it, but he wasn't fast enough. Within seconds it had him, oozing up his body, trapping him, as if he were wrapped in a blanket of the strongest glue.

He wanted to cry out to the mysterious woman, who still sat upon the rock, but the darkness had slithered up to cover his mouth, taking away his voice.

"Now you see what it has become," she said quietly, seemingly unaffected by his calamity. It was the last thing he heard before the liquid black stole away all his senses.

"You're not going to get me," Tom grunted as he thrashed his arms, struggling to break free. Finally, he threw off the covers and tumbled from the bed onto the hard wooden floor of his bedroom.

"What the heck was that all about?" Roderick asked as he rubbed sleep from his eyes.

Tom sat on the floor, stunned.

The raccoon dropped down to squat beside him. "Are you all right, Tom?"

"Yeah, I'm fine," he said, still reeling from the memory of his nightmare.

In the gloom of early morning, he found his way to the small table and lit the candle. Then he started to get dressed.

"What are you doin' now?" Roderick wanted to know. "It's not even morning."

"I don't want to go back to sleep," the boy said, and truer words were never spoken. There was no way he wanted to chance winding up back in the Dreaming with that spooky woman and the darkness that had attacked him.

"So what are you gonna do?" the raccoon asked.

The boy shrugged as he buckled the belt of his tunic around his waist. "I don't know; maybe I'll go to the fields early, get a head start on the day."

"Might as well," Roderick said, slapping his furry cheeks to wake himself up a bit more. "Bet that'll make your dad happy."

"Yeah, it probably will," Tom agreed. He found his lantern and lit the wick. "Let's go," he said, moving toward the door. "And be extra quiet; we don't want to wake anybody up."

"Hey, Tom," Roderick whispered. He was holding Tom's sword. "Do you think we might need this?"

Tom shook his head. "Nah, leave it here. I don't think I'll need it to pick turnips."

The two crept from the house, the sound of Tom's parents' snoring following them out into the gloomy haze that came just before sunrise. For most of the way, they walked in silence, Roderick sticking close to the light thrown by his friend's lantern.

"So what was your dream about?" the raccoon finally asked.

"It was pretty scary," the boy admitted as he trudged along the woodland path. "I was in this place called the Dreaming, and there was this strange lady."

"Who was she?"

"I don't know, but I got the idea that she used to live there, until something bad happened . . . something called the Nacht."

"The Nacht," Roderick repeated in a whisper. "That does sound scary."

"Not only does it *sound* scary, it *is* scary," the boy assured him. "You shoulda seen it, Roderick. It was like the darkness was swallowing everything up."

The raccoon stopped short. "But the Nacht isn't real . . . right?" he asked, his voice squeaking nervously.

Tom started to tell him that it wasn't, but something stopped him, something told him he would be lying if he were to say no.

"Let's hope not," he finally answered.

He lifted his lantern to see how close they were to the turnip fields. He thought they should have been there by now, but the forest around him looked strangely unfamiliar.

"That's odd," he said.

"What?" Roderick asked. "What's odd?" He jumped closer to Tom and peered out from behind one of Tom's legs.

"I think we might've gone off the path," Tom said, still moving his lantern around, trying to find something — anything — that looked familiar.

"Off the path? How could we have done that?" the raccoon asked. "We've walked this way hundreds of times."

"I know, but I don't recognize anything," the boy said, walking a little bit farther just to be sure. "Nope, I don't know where we are. Maybe if we head back this way . . ." He caught movement in the glow of the lantern and lifted it higher.

"What do you see, Tom?" Roderick asked, scampering over to stand beside him.

"I thought I saw something moving."

Tom slowly panned the light across the area and saw that something was rising up from the forest floor — a figure made from rock, dirt, roots, bark, and leaves.

A creature made of the forest.

"Are you seeing this?" Roderick asked, pinching Tom's leg.

He was seeing it all right, and once the being was fully formed, it spoke.

"Hello, Tom," it said in a voice like the rustling of leaves in the wind.

CHAPTER 6

Percival F. Bone remembered.

He had been there that night, at the special meeting of the Boneville Explorers' Society, as had his brother and his brother's wife — the twins' parents.

That special night when the Bone cousins — Fone Bone, Phoney Bone, and Smiley Bone — talked about their adventures in a mysterious place called the Valley.

They had become the darlings of Boneville upon their return, appearing on all the talk shows and giving lectures to anybody who would listen to their extraordinary adventures. Smiley had even written a bestselling memoir about his time away.

Yes, everybody had loved the Bone cousins and their stories . . . everybody except the members of the Boneville Explorers' Society.

The cousins had come to the meeting that night hoping

to convince the Society that what they had experienced in the Valley was true. They had even brought a supposed Rat Creature cub along.

What had its name been? Percival wondered. *Bartleby?* It hadn't looked like a ferocious creature to him, just some kind of dog perhaps.

Most of the old-time Bone adventurers and explorers attending the special gathering had found it all incredibly amusing — the tales of unknown kingdoms and magic, of dragons and hairy beasts called Rat Creatures. The Society thought it was all too far-fetched, and refused to believe the cousins no matter how many times they crossed their hearts or swore on a copy of *Moby-Dick*.

The Bone cousins had left the meeting that night, ridiculed by the Explorers' Society. But Percival had seen the look in his brother's eyes. Norman and Emmy Bone had listened to the stories with a rapt gaze that told Percival they believed . . . and that they were headed for adventure.

Within a matter of days, the twins' parents were ready, having put together an expedition by using what information they could get from the Bone cousins' stories to plot their course.

Percival had done everything he could to convince them to stay home, but the fire in their eyes was too strong. And

Percival, of all people, knew when that fire was burning — that hungry yearning for adventure — nothing could put it out.

Norman and Emmy said their farewells, shaking Percival's hand and kissing their children, with a promise to return with proof that the Valley did indeed exist.

They were never heard from again.

Lying upon the hard, wooden deck, Percival felt the *Queen of the Sky* roll beneath him, the mighty craft creaking and moaning as it listed from one side to the other.

It was peacefully quiet after the storm.

"The storm!" Percival exclaimed, eyes flying open as he suddenly remembered what had happened. "Abbey! Barclay!" he called out. He climbed quickly to his feet and searched for signs of his niece and nephew, finding only a good portion of his supplies and the crates they had been in smashed and strewn across the deck.

His heart hammered in his chest as he ran toward the wheelhouse.

"Abbey! Barclay! Where are you?" he shouted, peering through the glass into a dark and empty room. He watched the *Queen*'s large steering wheel spin slowly from left to right, as if driven by ghostly hands. But he knew there were no spirits involved here, just an automatic piloting system programmed to kick in during times of emergency.

During times very much like this.

Percival felt sick with panic as he left the wheelhouse. "Abbey! Barclay!" he screamed again.

"Please, Unc, not so loud," Barclay groaned as he popped up from inside a crate that had managed to remain intact. "I got a really bad headache."

"Barclay!" Percival grabbed the boy under the arms and hauled him from the box. "Are you all right?" He patted him over to make sure that nothing was broken.

"I'm fine," Barclay said, trying to squirm away. "I think Abbey kicked me in the head when the storm —"

"Abbey," Percival gasped. "Where is she?"

The boy looked around. "I thought she was inside the box with me," he said, puzzled.

"Oh no." Percival resumed his search of the deck for the little girl. "Abbey!" he called out. "Abbey, where are you?" He tossed aside broken pieces of wood and other wreckage from the storm, afraid of what he might find.

"Abbey!" Barclay yelled, hands cupped to his mouth. "Uncle Percival is gonna be really mad if he thinks you're dead and you're really not."

"Who says I'm dead?" Abbey's voice called out as she emerged from the wheelhouse, her arms filled with blankets.

Percival turned just in time to see the door of the wheelhouse swing out and strike Barclay in the behind, launching him across the deck toward the side of the ship.

The Bone adventurer dove and managed to grab hold of the back of Barclay's pants, stopping him just as he was about to go over the edge.

"Whoa!" the boy cried.

Percival took a peek as he hauled the boy back onto the deck and had to agree. The *Queen of the Sky* was flying above the clouds at her maximum altitude, land very far below indeed.

"Thanks, Uncle Percy," Barclay said. "I probably wouldn't have hit bottom 'til next Tuesday."

"Nah," Percival said with a relieved smile. "Probably more like Monday afternoon, about three-ish." He affectionately rubbed the boy's head before turning his attention to Abbey.

"Abbey Bone, you had me worried sick!" Percival said. "Where on earth have you been?"

"I knew the storm didn't take her," Barclay muttered. "And if it did, it probably woulda brought her back, she's such a pain."

"Hush, Barclay," Percival scolded. "Where were you, Abbey? Didn't you hear us calling?"

Abbey dropped the pile of blankets to the deck. "I was below deck in the supply room," she explained. "When

I woke up, it felt chilly, so I figured we could use some blankets."

"I'm glad you're okay," Percival said, and gave her a hug and a kiss on the top of her head. "And you're right, it is chilly."

They each grabbed a blanket and threw it over their shoulders.

"We've got some cleaning up to do, but why don't we see about bringing the *Queen* down a little lower first. Maybe we can warm things up a bit and figure out where we are."

"Aye, aye, Captain!" Barclay announced, giving his uncle a salute. Then he ran into the wheelhouse, blanket trailing behind him like a cape.

"Don't touch anything!" Percival ordered, following the boy inside.

"He better not," Abbey warned, joining them. "That's all we need, is him breaking something."

"I ain't gonna break nothin'," Barclay exclaimed.

"Good boy," Percival said as he took his position before the wheel. There were some knobs and switches on a fancy control panel to the right of the wheel; he reached down to give them a turn and a flip. A bell clanged loudly three times, and he smiled.

The captain was in control of the *Queen*.

"All right, then." While gripping the wheel in one hand,

he reached up to grab hold of a knob above his head. When turned to the right, it closed the burner, allowing the gas in the balloons to cool and the *Queen* to descend. "Let's take her down."

The sky craft began to drop, passing through the cottony clouds. Percival could already feel the temperature rising, and he shucked off his blanket.

"That's better," he said with a grin.

The twins did the same and raced out of the wheelhouse for a peek at their new surroundings.

"Can't wait to see where the storm took us," Abbey said, pushing her brother out of the way so she could see first. "Bet we're a hundred miles from Boneville."

"I bet we're even more than that," Barclay said. "I bet we're five hundred miles from Boneville."

Percival chuckled, still holding the wheel as he watched the kids peer over the port side of the sky ship.

"Well?" he called out. "Who's right?"

Strangely, neither responded.

"Hey, kids," Percival called, but still they were quiet, which was unusual. Maybe they couldn't hear him over the wind.

Percival placed the *Queen* on autopilot and left the controls.

"Didn't you hear me?" he asked, sidling up beside them. "I asked who was right." Then he looked over the side of the

Queen of the Sky and understood why they'd been stricken speechless.

They were floating over a vast desert, heading toward a formation of cruel-looking mountains. And beyond those mountains — just about coming into view — was a valley.

"I don't think either of us was right," Abbey whispered.

"I think we're a lot more than five hundred miles away from Boneville," Barclay added.

"Where are we, Uncle Percival?" Abbey asked.

The Valley, he thought, in total awe. *The storm somehow brought us to the Valley.*

Randolf Clearmeadow knew it was a lie but wished with all his heart that it was true.

He was standing before the home that he'd built for his family with his own two hands. It had been made from large rocks he'd pulled from a stream not far from his property, and the roof was laid with thick, yellow thatch. He'd used smaller stones to make the chimney that now belched a sweet-smelling smoke into the twilight sky.

Perhaps Ilana is making bread, Randolf thought happily. He moved toward the peaceful dwelling as a small figure emerged, wearing a pretty blue dress made by her mother. A crown of wildflowers adorned her golden hair.

"Daddy!" his daughter cried out, throwing open her arms as she ran at him.

"Corey," he said softly, his heart lifting. He ran to meet her, but no matter how far or how fast he ran, Randolf couldn't get any closer to the little girl. And then Ilana, his wife, came out of the house, wiping her hands on a towel. She smiled when she saw him in the distance.

Randolf grunted with exertion and frustration as he tried to run faster, feeling more and more hopeless that he would ever reach them. Ilana took Corey's hand and they stood together, waving and calling out to him, but he couldn't make out what they were saying over the growing rumble of thunder.

Roiling gray clouds suddenly filled the sky. It was full-on night now, but the flashes of lightning made it look as though dawn was arriving in short bursts of searing white.

Randolf was filled with dread as he realized what this night was, and why it was all a lie. He hadn't been home *that* night of lightning. He'd been out, performing the duties of the Veni Yan, leaving his family alone. Leaving his family at the mercy of . . .

In a flash of light he saw them, large and fearsome, their bodies covered in thick, dirty fur.

The Hairy Men . . . Rat Creatures.

They skulked around the edge of the forest and clung to the black shadows, nearly invisible until their presence was revealed in a white flash of the approaching storm.

"No!" Randolf cried, his heart beating furiously, but his words were swallowed by a deafening crack of thunder. His family continued to wave happily, little Corey even blowing him kisses.

The night sky brightened with jagged bolts of Heaven's fury, revealing the monsters stalking across the yard toward his unsuspecting family. "Run!" he screamed at them, but they only continued to smile and laugh, waving him home.

Randolf fell to the ground. He closed his eyes, wishing he could pretend that it all had never happened.

The Rat Creatures moved with incredible speed, first snatching away his wife and then his beautiful little girl. One second they were there, happy as ever, and the next — they were gone.

As if they'd never been there at all.

They didn't even have a chance to scream, so Randolf Clearmeadow screamed for them.

The two Rat Creatures were running for their lives.

"Do you see?" the Rat Creature who had been snuggled by the King asked as they raced through the winding passage, a pack of Agak's soldiers in close pursuit. "Do you see the trouble your stupid dead squirrel has caused?"

The Rat Creature with the prized treasure was silent as he ran, the sounds of the King's loyal legion — those who wouldn't dream of taking their leader's food — snarling and snapping behind them. He continued to tightly clutch his precious booty. After all he'd been through to get it back, he wasn't about to let it go.

"Don't blame my squirrel," the Rat Creature finally snapped. "It's not his fault that he just so happens to be the most delicious dead tree rodent in all the land." He held the rotting carcass up to his face. "Isn't that right, Fredrick?"

"Fredrick?" his comrade screamed. "Why are you calling it Fredrick?"

"I thought he should have a name."

"WE don't even have names," the Other Rat Creature bellowed.

"That's because nobody thinks we're special," the Rat Creature answered, a quiver of sadness in his voice.

The light of day appeared in the cave opening ahead.

"When we're not being chased by the King's minions . . ." the Rat Creature's companion began.

"Yes?"

"Remind me to smash your head with a rock."

"I don't think that's very nice at all," the Rat Creature commented as they escaped into the daylight. "And neither does Fredrick."

CHAPTER 7

Tom wished he'd brought his sword.

He knew very well that it was only a stick, but at least he would have had something to protect himself from the strange creature that had taken shape before them.

"It knows your name, Tom," Roderick squeaked as he hid behind his friend. "How does it know your name?"

"I . . . I . . . don't know," Tom stammered, unable to take his eyes from the figure before him.

"Don't you remember me, Tom?" it asked in a woman's voice.

"Do . . . do I know you?" Tom stammered.

"We met briefly," the forest woman said. She stretched out arms made from woven roots and vines, and wiggled fingers made of twigs. "But I suppose I did look different then."

She waved her hand over the ground beneath her, and up grew a chair made of rock.

"You're the sad lady from my dream!" Tom gasped, the realization hitting him hard. "She's the one I was telling you about, Roderick."

"I think she's more scary than sad," the raccoon commented, peering out from between the boy's legs.

The forest woman slowly lowered herself down upon the rock seat. "I apologize for my appearance," she said. "But it has been some time since I last wore the form you saw in your vision."

"Vision?" Roderick asked. "You had a vision, Tom?"

"I think she means the stuff she showed me in my dream," he explained. "Right?" he asked her.

"Exactly right, Tom," she answered with a nod, the green leaves of her hair rustling. "I used your dream to show you something of grave importance . . . something that could affect the lives of everyone in this valley." She paused, her dark, pebble eyes looking about her. "And possibly even the whole wide world."

"Why me?" Tom asked. "What are you showing it to me for? I'm just a kid."

"But you are a special child," the forest woman said, pointing at him with a long, gnarled finger of wood. A beetle crawled on the end of it, its wings buzzing as it flew away.

"Do you hear that, Tom?" Roderick asked. "She says you're special."

Tom heard, but he still didn't understand.

"Who are you?" he asked. "What are you?"

"Pardon my rudeness," she said, standing up. She placed a hand upon her chest and bowed her leafy head. "I am Lorimar of the First Folk," she announced. "And the last, I fear, of my kind."

"The First Folk?" Tom asked. "I've never heard of them. . . . Who are they?"

"We were creatures of the Dreaming, living in perfect harmony with that spirit world until the Lord of Locusts decided to move into the realm of humans. He took possession of the first Dragon . . . our beloved Queen Mim."

Lorimar paused a moment before going on.

"The Queen was overcome by madness, and the balance of the Dreaming was thrown into chaos. The First Folk tried to help, but we were no match for the Queen under the Locust's sway. Most of us were destroyed. It was up to the other Dragons then."

"That's how the Valley came to be, right?" Roderick spoke up. "There was a big fight and stuff."

Lorimar lifted her head, fixing the raccoon in her gaze as if seeing him for the first time. "Yes, it was, little forest creature," she said. "And who might you be?"

"This is Roderick," Tom said. "He's my friend."

"Hello, friend Roderick." The woman bowed toward him and then continued her tale. "As the Dragons battled their possessed queen, their terrible struggles shaped this very land. Eventually, the Dragons defeated Queen Mim by trapping her — and the Lord of Locusts — in stone forever."

"What happened to the Dreaming? Was it okay?" Tom asked.

"If only it was," Lorimar uttered with a sigh. "But chaos continued to reign in the Dreaming. The surviving First Folk did everything they could to make things right, but there was another . . . a servant of the Locust Lord . . . a Dragon that had gone against his brethren. He called himself the Nacht."

Tom felt an icy finger run down his spine at the mention of the name.

"Before his dragon brothers and sisters could defeat him, he took revenge upon the First Folk. He struck at our already diminished numbers, destroying those of us who survived."

"But you're not destroyed . . . you managed to get away," Tom said, captivated by the chilling tale.

"I managed to escape to the Waking World, where I hoped to warn the other dragons of the Nacht's treachery, but I was too late. The Queen, and the Locust Lord possessing her, had already been imprisoned in stone, and the Dragons had returned to the earth."

"What happened then?" Roderick asked.

"I was weak from my journey, so I let my spirit merge with these new surroundings so that I might rest and recover, and someday . . ."

Lorimar grew very still and silent.

"You never got to go back, did you?" Tom asked, sensing why the forest woman was so sad.

She shook her head, again stirring the leaves of her long, green hair.

"I slept for a very long time," she said. "I lost myself in the elements of the forest, and I would have continued this sleep if something hadn't disturbed my slumber . . . something terrible."

Roderick became excited. "I bet she's talkin' about the fight for the Valley, when the Lord of the Locusts tried to come back."

"Right before Thorn was crowned," Tom added, feeling a surge of pride as he spoke the new Queen's name.

"You're right," Lorimar said. "But even after the Locust was again defeated and peace spread throughout the Valley . . . something equally dangerous was stirring."

Tom knew where this was all leading.

"The Nacht has come back, hasn't he?" Tom said, trying not to let his voice give away his fear. He didn't want to scare Roderick.

"I believed he had fled," Lorimar continued. "Retreating to the dangerous, shadowy void that exists between the Dreaming and the Waking World . . . but he has returned. Sensing his master's second defeat, the Nacht has decided to strike at both the Dreaming *and* the Waking World."

Lorimar turned her full attention to Tom, her small stone eyes glistening wetly.

And Tom was suddenly very scared.

"Why are you looking at me that way?" Tom asked, wary of what the woman was going to say next.

"The Dreaming has chosen you as its agent against the Nacht," Lorimar said.

Tom shook his head furiously. "Sorry, but you must be mistaken. I'm just the son of a turnip farmer. . . . Tell her, Roderick."

"He's the son of a turnip farmer all right," the raccoon agreed, nodding.

"Son of a turnip farmer or not, you have been chosen," Lorimar said, rising from her seat of stone and flowing toward him.

"Why do you say that?" Tom asked, backing away. "How do you know this?"

Lorimar stopped and pointed at him. "The object around your neck," she hissed. Tom touched his lucky stone.

"This?" he asked. "This is just my lucky rock."

"Oh, it's much more than that," Lorimar said.

She reached out, gently scraping one of her long, twig fingers across the mysterious stone's rough black surface. The outer layer crumbled away to reveal a powerful glow, as if a fire burned within it.

"Hey, what did you do?" Tom asked, staring at the light. He suddenly remembered his dream, and how the stone had started to glow.

"I've only scratched away some of the darkness that has collected upon this fragment of Spark," Lorimar explained.

"Look at that," Roderick said dreamily. "So bright and pretty." The raccoon reached up for the stone.

Tom slapped his friend's paw away and returned his full attention to Lorimar. "So just because I have this rock . . . or Spark, or whatever you want to call it, I'm chosen?"

"Exactly." Lorimar clasped her hands before her. "I knew you would understand."

"No." Tom shook his head. "I don't understand."

"The Spark found you," Lorimar said. "It has picked *you* to be the one who makes it complete, and once that is done —"

"I don't know what it is, and I don't want to know!" Tom tore the rock from his neck and threw it on the ground.

Roderick immediately went to it, drawn to the white light that blazed from the jagged scratch on the stone's surface.

"Get away from that, Roderick," Tom warned. He grabbed the animal and pulled him back. "It's bad."

"No," Lorimar said softly. "It is something good, and powerful. Something that will help defeat the Nacht."

The forest woman bent down to retrieve Tom's stone.

"Before the Dreaming, there was only darkness," she said, carefully picking up the necklace and letting it dangle before her. "And then after a time came the most wondrous of lights. It pushed aside the black of nothing, and the Dreaming was born in a flash of creation."

The light leaking from the black rock danced upon her mossy face.

"This is but a tiny piece of that special light . . . a piece of the first spark that drove back the darkness."

"Wow," Roderick said, eyes wide in wonder. "I can't believe you found all that in a turnip. You're sooooooooooooo lucky, Tom."

But Tom wasn't feeling lucky. He just felt . . . wrong.

A part of him wanted to reach out and take his stone — *the Spark* — from Lorimar, but another part of him wanted to get as far away from it as possible.

He felt like the forest was closing in on him, the shadows creeping closer. This is what he imagined his life would become if he took the necklace back. There would only be fear, and darkness, and shadows.

Lorimar held the Spark out to him.

"Take it, Tom," she said, her voice like a gentle summer breeze. "Take it back, for it has chosen you to make it whole."

Tom's heart beat wildly in his chest as he slowly backed away. "I don't want it."

And suddenly the fear became so great that he was running . . . so great that he didn't even wait for Roderick.

Tom could hear his friend calling him, but he couldn't slow down. He had no idea where he was going — all he knew was that he had to get as far away from the Spark as possible.

Tree limbs reached down to scratch at his face and snag his clothes, and then his foot caught upon an ancient root, and Tom tumbled to the forest floor. He struggled to stand but couldn't find his footing in his panic.

And then he heard something coming.

Leaves and twigs crunched and snapped as it swiftly moved through the woods. It was coming for him, and all he could do was wait. He held his breath and . . .

Roderick sprang from the woods.

"What are you running away for?" the raccoon asked breathlessly.

Tom's eyes darted from left to right. "Afraid" was all he could manage through chattering teeth.

Carefully, Roderick stepped forward and took his friend's hand. "It's okay, Tom," he said. "Lorimar isn't chasing you. There's no reason to be afraid. I'm here . . . I'll protect you. Why don't we go in the house and tell your folks. . . ."

Tom blinked and looked around as the raccoon's words finally started to register. "The house?" he asked.

Roderick tugged on his hand, leading him into the clearing. "Yeah, the house; we're right here."

What had just moments before been totally foreign was now wonderfully familiar. Tom stepped from the woods and realized that the sun had risen in the sky, chasing away the frightening shadows. He was home.

"Mom! Dad!" he called out, beginning to run.

He wanted to tell them everything: about his strange dreams, the lucky rock that wasn't a rock — and not at all lucky, come to think of it — and the strange woman made from pieces of the forest.

He threw open the door and was immediately struck by the utter silence.

"Mom? Dad?" Tom called. "Lottie?"

"Maybe they've already gone to the fields," Roderick suggested, scampering in behind him.

"No," Tom answered. "The cart is still by the side of the house."

He went to his parents' room and rapped on the door with a knuckle. "Mom? Dad? Are you in here?" he asked as he pushed open the door.

His parents were still in bed, sound asleep, his father's heavy breathing like the bellows used to fan the fires in the hearth.

Tom reached out and gave them each a good shake. "It's time to get up," he said, raising his voice a bit. "C'mon, wake up, you're gonna be late to the fields." If anything was going to wake his parents, it would be the turnip fields.

But still they slept.

"Are they up?" Roderick asked from the doorway.

"No," Tom answered. "I can't seem to wake them."

The raccoon disappeared, and Tom guessed that he was checking on Lottie.

"Mom . . . Dad, wake up!" he yelled at the top of his lungs, shaking them violently.

His father's mouth opened wider as he continued to snore, and something caught Tom's eye. It moved quickly, snaking up out of his father's open mouth, before disappearing back inside.

A shadow. A shadow moving like it was alive.

Tom gasped and jumped away from the bed.

"Lottie won't wake up either," Roderick said, darting into the room. "I pinched her nose and everything. What're we gonna do?"

The fear was back, only this time Tom knew what he was afraid of.

The Nacht.

"Tom Elm!" a voice cried out, startling the friends.

"It came from outside," Roderick said, dropping to all fours and running for the front door, Tom close behind.

The door was still open just a crack, and Tom could see a strangely familiar, flickering light creeping in. He held his breath as he pulled the doorknob.

Lorimar stood before him, light pouring from the piece of the Spark that dangled from her branchlike fingers.

"There's something wrong with my parents," Tom cried.

"The Nacht's power is growing here; he's extending his evil reach beyond the Dreaming into the Waking World."

"Can you help them?" he asked plaintively, trying hard not to cry.

"I cannot," Lorimar said, "but you can."

"I . . . I'm afraid," he told the forest woman. He couldn't explain it, but it felt like a paralyzing fear had overtaken his entire body.

"It is the Nacht you sense," Lorimar said, allowing the

fragment of Spark to sway hypnotically in her grasp. "The Nacht has taken hold of your fear and is using it against you."

"I don't know what to do," Tom said, his voice cracking with despair as he thought about his family.

"Take back the Spark," Lorimar said. "Drive back the darkness with light."

"If I take it, will it help my parents and my sister?" he asked, terrified of what the answer might be.

"Take it and you will see," the forest woman urged him. "But decide quickly. . . ."

She turned her leafy head toward the ring of woods around the Elm property. There were things moving in the shadows, things emerging into the morning light.

Things that shouldn't have been moving at all.

They were animals, but not just any animals. These were dead. Their fur was matted and, in some instances, missing — rotted away to expose dry muscle and yellow bone. But they were moving, stiffly crawling toward them.

"Are you seeing what I'm seeing?" Roderick squeaked.

"Yes," Tom said, watching in revulsion.

"Those animals . . . those animals are dead, right?" his raccoon friend asked.

"They sure look that way," Tom answered.

"Then why are they moving?"

He was about to answer when he saw it, creeping from a dead rabbit's mouth to slither into a ragged hole in its side. Living shadow, just like Tom had seen in his father's mouth.

Then, as if things weren't bad enough, the rabbit began to speak.

"Do not take this quest," it said in a voice that made the hair on Tom's arms and the back of his neck stand on end.

"You're just a little boy," said a dead possum, its eye sockets filled with squirming black shadow. "Who knows what sort of horrible things could happen to you."

Lorimar turned toward the creeping animal corpses, letting the light of the Spark shine in their direction. They stopped abruptly and shielded their decaying faces.

"Put that thing away!" the rabbit screeched.

"Back beneath the cold, dark earth where it belongs," added a bird whose wings were missing most of their feathers, showing only spindly bones.

Lorimar glanced over her shoulder at Tom.

"Do you see the Spark's power now, Tom?" she asked. "If you were to retrieve all of its pieces, the Nacht could be permanently expelled from this world, as well as from the Dreaming."

Tom saw, but it didn't change the fact that he was just

a kid. What could *he* do against something as powerful and scary as the Nacht?

"Can't somebody else take it?" he asked. "How about Roderick?"

"I don't want it!" the raccoon exclaimed.

The dead animals laughed.

"You've got it right, boy," something that might once have been a deer croaked. "Why would you want something like that? . . . It can only lead to bad things."

Tom knew what they were trying to do. If what Lorimar had told him was true, the Spark had chosen him, and only him. If he didn't take it, then the Nacht would win, and his folks would never wake up.

"Give it to me!" he said quickly, before he could change his mind.

"Don't do it, boy," a porcupine whose head was just a bare skull warned.

"If you know what's good for you," finished a fat woodchuck that looked like it had only recently died.

The animals surged forward, despite the light, as if sensing that their attempts to sway him were not working.

"Is that what you want?" Lorimar asked, still directing the light of the Spark at the encroaching dead.

Tom shook his head. "Not at all, but I don't have a choice," he said. "If I don't do this, my family is going to suffer."

"That's the bravest thing I ever heard," Roderick said, giving Tom's leg a quick hug.

"Or the stupidest," the boy replied.

Tom stepped toward the forest woman and held out his hand.

"I'll take that," he said.

"Don't do it, Tom Elm!" all the rotting creatures cried as one.

But Tom didn't listen. Slowly he reached out and wrapped his hand around the body of the stone, the light growing more intense as his fingers closed around it.

And then came a flash so bright it was as if the sun had appeared in his front yard.

CHAPTER 8

The *Queen of the Sky* floated above the lush Valley forest. They had been exploring all through the night, and now the morning sun was eagerly rising over the horizon.

Percival stifled a yawn as he panned the beam of the sky ship's spotlight over the tops of the trees below. "Looks like we're gonna need two more potatoes, Barclay," he called out to his nephew as he noticed the light of the lamp dimming.

He opened a door set into the side of the spotlight to peer at its mechanical guts. The two potatoes, hooked up to multiple copper wires inside the casing, were a little on the unfresh side.

Not hearing any movement behind him, Percival turned and found his nephew wrapped in a blanket, curled up beside his sister, both fast asleep.

He smiled. *They are awfully cute*, he thought, closing the spotlight canister. He would get some fresh spuds later. For now, the dawn's early light would help him see.

The adventurer inside him could barely contain itself. Looking out into the distance, Percival imagined the unknown thrills and potential dangers that awaited him below. He wanted nothing more than to land the *Queen of the Sky* and explore.

Behind him, Abbey murmured something about blueberries, and Barclay let out a honking snort, and Percival was reminded why he had yet to throw himself into the thick of things. He had responsibilities now. If something were to happen to him, who would look after the twins?

No, he had to control himself, and explore responsibly.

He took a few deep breaths and gazed out over the treetops. *I can do this*, he thought, showing his excitement who was boss. He would take things slowly. There was plenty of time to —

A blinding flash of brilliant light came from somewhere in the forest below. Multiple colored dots were suddenly doing the tango before his eyes.

"Thar she blows!" Percival yelled at the top of his lungs, already on the move. He rushed into the wheelhouse and spun the release valve to drop the *Queen* toward the site of the flash.

He couldn't resist. This wasn't just the call of adventure anymore, it was a scream. This was a *Get down here right now, Percival F. Bone, and have a great big slice of adventure pie.*

"What is it, Uncle Percy?" Abbey asked, suddenly awake. She threw off her blanket and ran to look over the side of the *Queen.*

"Is it time for school already?" Barclay asked dreamily, and then smacked his gums. He looked around, getting his bearings, eyes still glazed from sleep.

"You might say that it is," Percival said, as the ship dropped closer to the ground.

"Welcome to your first day of class at the school of adventure."

The Rat Creatures were hiding beneath a bush when the flash of light occurred.

"Don't you worry about a thing, Fredrick," the Rat Creature said, stroking the matted fur of the dead squirrel.

"Did you see that?" the Other Rat Creature asked, lifting his shaggy head to peek out at the woods around them. "Did you see that flash?"

"No," the Rat Creature replied. "Fredrick and I were —"

"Shut up about Fredrick," the Other Rat snapped angrily. "That's just a dead squirrel, not your best friend."

"I don't know what's gotten into you," the Rat Creature declared, clutching the dead animal to his furry chest.

"What did Fredrick do to you?"

"What did Fredrick do to me?" the Other screeched. "He's got us into trouble with the King . . . the kind of trouble that we could end up dead for. That's what Fredrick's done to me."

"I think you're jealous," the Rat Creature blurted. "You see how close Freddy and I have grown in such a short period of time and —"

"Freddy?" the Other Rat asked in disbelief.

"Isn't that cute?" the Rat Creature asked, a goofy grin stretching from ear to ear. "He loves it when I call him that."

"I think I'm done talking about this," the Other Rat Creature said, and began to crawl from the shelter of the bush.

"Where are you going?" his friend asked. "The King's soldiers might see you."

"I want to check out that flash," the Other said. "Who knows, maybe Agak's minions have been struck by lightning, and we no longer have anything to worry about."

"But . . . what if you're wrong?"

The Other Rat was silent, half of his body already out in the open.

"Then I guess you and Fredrick will be very happy together," he said, leaving the hiding place, and his comrade, behind.

"I knew you were jealous!" the Rat Creature screeched as he scrambled to follow, the dead squirrel clutched protectively in his shaggy paw.

Randolf fought to free himself of the nightmare's hold.

It was like swimming up through thick, black tar, the viscous liquid doing everything it could to suffocate him. But no matter how worthless he had felt since losing his family, he would not allow himself to be defeated, and found the strength to escape the oppressive dream.

The Veni Yan awoke with a gasp.

After the incident in the tavern, he had been placed in a jail cell in the Constable's quarters. Now he was kneeling upon the cold, stone floor, coughing and sputtering as if he'd been drowning.

But this wasn't water — it was tendrils of darkness that dripped from his nose and mouth, that spattered to the floor before slithering out of his cell like serpents.

Randolf had never seen anything like it, and watched dumbfounded as they wound their way across the floor toward the sleeping Constable Roarke and his deputies.

"Hey!" he cried out as he clambered to his feet. "Wake up . . . hey!"

They didn't hear him, and the nightmare serpents slithered up the bodies of the still-sleeping lawmen.

"Listen to me!" he screamed again, hands clutching the

cold bars of his prison cell. "You need to wake up!"

But still they slept, and the shadows made their way between the men's parted lips and into their nostrils.

The men began to twitch and moan as if having a bad dream.

Randolf helplessly watched from his cell, as one by one the Constable and his deputies awoke.

No longer the men they were when they'd fallen asleep.

CHAPTER 9

Tom was surprised that it didn't hurt. He'd expected his hand to burn when he touched the stone, but instead it sort of tickled and sent an odd tingling sensation through his entire body. All the dirt and grime that had made the Spark look like some plain old rock had flaked away, and the full intensity of the light shone through.

The flash was blinding; he blinked away the colored spots that floated before his eyes.

And as his vision began to clear, he saw things.

Images that he couldn't really explain appeared, flashes of people, places, and things that he did not recognize but somehow knew he would when the time came.

The first thing he saw was the Kingdom of Atheia; he'd gone there with his parents to see the coronation of Queen Thorn. But the great city appeared much different now from the way it had then. It was unusually quiet . . . silent as the grave.

Tom suddenly knew — he felt it in his belly — that he'd be traveling there again to help the Kingdom, traveling south to help the Queen.

Thorn.

Atheia was swiftly replaced by a vision of three strange-looking creatures dropping out of the sky in a floating ship. The vision quickly shifted to an older man wearing the old and tattered robes of a warrior priest, trapped in a jail cell, and then just as quickly to the startling sight of two loathsome Rat Creatures emerging from the forest. *Was that a dead squirrel one of them carried?*

Then, as quickly as they were upon him, the images were gone, and Tom found himself back in the front yard of his home. He was still clutching the shard of Spark, and it pulsed warmly like a tiny heartbeat in his hand.

Without any question, he placed the necklace back around his neck and looked about the yard. The dead animals that had been creeping menacingly toward them were once again lifeless, their decaying forms steaming in the morning sun. Tom imagined that the brilliant flash from the Spark must have driven the Nacht's evil spirits from the animals' bodies.

Roderick and Lorimar quickly approached him.

"You okay, Tom?" his furry friend asked with concern.

"When you grabbed the Spark and it flashed like that, I thought for sure you might be . . ."

"It was the strangest thing," Tom began excitedly. "I saw images of Atheia inside my head, and I knew that the Queen was in trouble. And then I saw these little white creatures —"

"Were they Bones?" Roderick asked excitedly. "I like Bones!"

"I think they were," Tom agreed. "And I think I saw a Veni Yan priest who was in jail. And you're not gonna like this, Roderick, but there were these two Rat Creatures, and . . . oh yeah, those Bones I was telling you about? They had a ship, only this one was able to sail in the air and —"

But his friends weren't paying any attention; they were staring up into the sky.

"What's the matter? What are you looking at?" Tom asked, turning around to crane his neck, shielding his eyes from the glare of the sun.

"A sky ship, you say?" Lorimar questioned.

"A sky ship like that one?" Roderick added, pointing up at the sky.

Tom was speechless, unable to take his eyes from the magnificent wooden ship floating above their heads.

"Just like that one," he finally managed, as the craft began to descend toward earth.

"Ahoy there!" a Bone called out with a friendly wave.

"Hello!" Tom returned the wave, noticing two Bone children peering over the side of the sky craft with cautious eyes.

Roderick started to jump up and down, excitedly waving both arms.

"The name is Percival F. Bone," the Bone with the really big nose said. "We're new to your valley and are having a look around."

"I'm Abbey, and we're explorers," the little girl Bone yelled down.

"We're going to the school of adventure, and I'm Barclay," the little boy Bone added.

"Greetings to you all. I'm Tom Elm, and these are my friends, Roderick and Lorimar. That's an amazing vessel you have there."

"This old thing?" Percival said with a chuckle. "She gets me where I need to go." He reached over and affectionately patted the ship's wooden hull.

"Are you peaceful?" Barclay asked them. "You're not gonna try and eat us or anything if we come down there, right?"

The little girl punched him. "What's wrong with you, asking stupid questions," she scolded the boy. "You ain't gonna eat us, right?" she then asked Tom.

He laughed. "We don't eat people here in the Valley," he told them.

"We don't, but those two Rat Creatures you saw in your vision might," Roderick muttered so only Tom could hear.

"Hush, Roderick," Tom told his friend. "I don't even know what that meant."

The sky vessel dropped closer, coming to a stop as its belly scraped against the tops of the trees.

"That's about as close as we can get," Percival called out. "We'll need to take the ladder down."

Tom heard some scuffling on the deck, and then a heavy, metal anchor attached to a rope dropped from the ship and thumped the earth. A rope ladder was tossed over next, stopping a few inches from the ground.

Abbey was first down the ladder, followed closely by Barclay. Percival was last, and he dropped to the ground with a wobble.

"Give me a sec to get my land legs back," he said, swaying a bit from side to side.

"Pleased to meetcha," he said after a moment, and stuck out his hand for Tom to shake. "We come in peace and all that business."

Tom shook his hand eagerly. "It's nice to meet you, too!"

"You're Bones!" Roderick said, pointing at them.

"And you're a raccoon," Percival added. "Tell me something I don't know."

"Do you know the Queen's best friend in the whole

wide world, Fone Bone?" Tom asked excitedly.

"Know 'im?" Percival said. "We're cousins on my father's side."

Lorimar folded her spindly wooden fingers before her. "Ah yes, Bones . . . a resilient species. The Dreaming has chosen wisely," she said.

"Chosen?" Percival asked. "Who got chosen?"

Tom could see the confusion on his new friend's face and tried to explain.

"There's this creature called the Nacht threatening to turn everything to darkness, and I was chosen by the Dreaming to find all the pieces of the first Spark."

Tom grabbed the glowing white rock from around his neck to show Percival. "See?"

But just as the words were leaving his lips, his mind again filled with images . . . another vision that the Dreaming wanted him — *needed* him — to see.

Tom saw the older man in the jail cell again . . . the Veni Yan priest. There were men . . . no, they used to be men, but now they were under the spell of the Nacht.

"What's wrong, kid?" Tom heard Percival ask, his voice sounding far away. "Are you having a fit or something?"

But Tom couldn't respond.

The Nacht's men were surrounding the jail cell, moving stiffly like the dead animals that had crawled from the woods. They were trying to get at the man locked inside.

And at once Tom knew what had to be done.

"We have to help him," he said, snapping back to the present.

"Help who?" Percival asked.

"There's a man who needs our help in the village of Trumble."

"Okay," Percival said, rubbing his chin in thought. "Who is this guy and why does he need us?"

"The Spark just showed me another vision," Tom explained. "He's supposed to be one of us . . . supposed to be joining us on our quest."

"Quest?" Percival questioned. "Now hold on a second. Who said anything about going on a quest?"

The twins started to cheer.

"Hooray! We're going on a quest!" they said in unison.

Roderick stepped closer, worry on his furry face. "If this guy needs our help, Trumble is at least a day's travel from here."

"Only if we're on foot," Tom said, looking at Percival hopefully.

"How else were you planning on —?" Roderick started, but suddenly understood when he saw the way Tom was staring at the Bone sky captain.

"Oh, I get it." The raccoon nodded.

"You're not suggesting we use . . ." Percival pointed to the sky craft floating in the air above their heads.

Tom, Roderick, and even Lorimar slowly nodded.

"It's the only way we can get there in time," Tom said.

"I don't know." Percival started to pace as he rubbed his chin.

"C'mon, Uncle Percy," Abbey said, pacing beside him. "We have to help this poor guy."

"This could be our first test at the school of adventure," Barclay suggested.

"I just don't know," the Bone explorer said. "It could be dangerous."

"It will be," Lorimar said flatly. "But nothing in comparison to what the world will be like if the Nacht is allowed to spread its evil."

Percival stopped pacing.

"I could really use your help," Tom said, hoping that the Spark's vision hadn't been a lie. "And we really need to move quickly." He waited, holding his breath.

"Oh, what the heck," the adventurer finally said, throwing his hands in the air. "Never really been on a quest before, and there's a first time for everything."

Roderick and the twins cheered and jumped around.

"But you're gonna fill me in on all the details as we fly. Deal?" Percival asked.

"Deal," Tom agreed, feeling a thrill of excitement tinged with fear as he realized that his life was about to change forever. And that the quest had already begun.

Tom carried his sleeping sister into their parents' room and laid her gently between them on the bed. He didn't want her to be alone.

As scared as he was of what might lay ahead, he knew that he had to do something . . . anything . . . to make them wake up again.

"I've got to go now," he told his sleeping family. "I'm going on a quest to try and help you and the rest of the Valley." He reached down and pulled the covers up beneath their chins.

"Hopefully, when I see you again, you guys'll be awake," he said, feeling the pressure of his task beginning to weigh on him. There was a lot at stake. The fate of his family — the whole Valley, really — depended on him. "And I can tell you all about what I saw and did, and introduce you to my new friends."

His father moaned as he rolled onto his side and then began to snore.

"I know I never say it, but I love you guys." Tom bent down and kissed them each upon the head.

"Are you ready, Tom?" He turned to see Roderick standing in the doorway. "Percival says we're set to go."

"I'm ready," Tom said, tearing his gaze away from his family and heading out the door.

. . .

"Let's get this show on the road!" Percival yelled to Tom and Roderick as they came from the house. He was holding on to the rope ladder that led to the *Queen of the Sky*.

The Bone adventurer glanced up at his ship. Everything seemed to be in working order. Abbey and Barclay had brought a fresh supply of potatoes from the hold, so they wouldn't be running out of power anytime soon. Yep, everything was good to go.

He felt the eyes of that strange woman, Lorimar, upon him and turned toward where she stood.

"We'll be under way soon as we're all aboard," the Bone said.

Lorimar's rock eyes shifted, looking into the dark woods around the house. "We must make haste if we are to rescue the newest member of our band from the growing evil of the Nacht."

"This Nacht is a real piece of work, I guess," Percival commented.

"Piece of work?" she repeated, not understanding his words.

"You know, a rotten egg, a no-goodnik, a lowlife."

She continued to stare.

He rubbed his chin, looking for just the right words.

"A bad guy!" he announced, and saw a look of understanding blossom upon her mossy face.

"Yes, the Nacht is a very bad man," Lorimar agreed. "And we will need to be strong to defeat him."

"Don't you worry another leaf on your head," Percival boasted, flexing a muscle in his arm. "Go ahead and feel that, go on. Solid like steel."

Again, Lorimar just looked at him.

"Never mind," he muttered as Tom and Roderick approached.

"Ready to climb aboard?" Percival asked, feeling his heartbeat quicken and the blood race through his veins.

"Ready," Tom said.

Percival looked to the raccoon. "How about you?"

"Ready!" Roderick said with a little jump of excitement.

"Great," the Bone explorer said, turning his attention to the mysterious woman.

"And you?"

Lorimar remained eerily quiet.

"Now, there's nothing to be afraid of," Percival encouraged, thinking she might need some reassurance. He reached out and gripped her elbow. It felt strange, as if he was holding on to a thick tree branch. "All you have to do is climb up this ladder and —"

Lorimar suddenly fell apart in his hands.

Percival was speechless as the forest lady just sort of crumbled before his eyes.

"I didn't do that!" he said, looking at the shocked expressions on the boy's and raccoon's faces.

"What happened?" Tom asked.

"She fell apart," Roderick said, approaching the pile of sticks, rock, leaves, and vines. He prodded it with one of his paws.

"I know she fell apart," the boy said. "But why? Isn't she supposed to go with us?"

"Don't know what to tell ya, kid," Percival said.

And there they stood, staring at the pile of forest litter, until one of the twins called down from the deck of the sky ship.

"Hey, I thought we were going on a quest!" Barclay yelled.

"Yeah, isn't there somebody who needs saving?" Abbey asked.

Tom looked away from Lorimar's remains. "Maybe she never intended to go with us," he said with a shrug. "I guess we should probably get going."

Percival stepped to the side of the ladder. "Then climb aboard, and let's get this show on the road!" He took one last look at the pile that had once been Lorimar and gave his head a shake. *What am I getting myself into?* he thought, then followed the boy and the raccoon up the ladder to the deck of the *Queen of the Sky*.

"Barclay! Abbey!" he bellowed as he climbed over the side.

"Yes, Captain!" the little Bones answered. They rushed across the deck and stopped at attention to deliver a salute.

"Bring up the ladder and anchor."

"Aye, aye, sir!" they announced, Abbey rushing to the side to retrieve the ladder, and Barclay to pull up the anchor.

"Hey, where's the plant lady?" Abbey asked.

"Don't ask." Percival headed toward the wheelhouse. "Make yourselves at home, boys," he said as he passed Tom and Roderick.

Percival grabbed the ship's wheel with one hand and reached up with the other to pull one of the cords that dangled above his head. This cord would turn up the burner, heating the gas and allowing them to rise.

Percival watched Tom's face through the wheelhouse window as the flame roared and the balloons filled with hot air. The boy's eyes were like saucers, and Percival knew exactly how he felt because he felt the same way every time he took the *Queen* up. He closed his eyes and sniffed at the air.

"Can you smell it?" he called out to them.

"What did you say?" Tom asked, coming to stand in the doorway.

"I asked if you could smell it," Percival said.

The boy sniffed the air with a nose that was tiny in comparison to Percival's.

"Smell what?" he finally asked.

"Adventure," Percival said, a sly smile snaking across his features as he gripped the wheel and steered the craft away. "The smell of adventure."

CHAPTER 10

The two Rat Creatures watched from the shadows of the woods.

"What is that?" one of them whispered, holding on to his dead squirrel all the tighter as he looked through the cover of some tall grass.

"I don't know," hissed the Other. "I've never seen anything like it."

But as frightened as they were, they could not tear their eyes from it. The object floated in the air like a big, wooden bird, and there were people on it . . . a fleshy human type, a woodland creature . . . and Bones.

Bones.

"Do you see what I see?" the Rat Creature asked, not believing his eyes. He even held up the squirrel so that it could see, too.

"Yes, I see," the Other responded. "It's like a giant wagon

that flies in the air. I've never seen anything like —"

"No, not the flying wagon, what's *on* the flying wagon." The Rat Creature pointed a long, clawed finger. "Look there."

The Other looked where his comrade was pointing and saw them . . . three in total.

"Bones," he said excitedly. "There are Bones on the flying wagon."

"Yes," the Rat said in deep contemplation as he stroked the mottled fur of his rotting rodent prize. An idea had started to form in the dark recesses of his tiny mind.

"A gift for the King," he said, turning his gaze to his companion.

The Other looked around suddenly. "Where?"

Again the Rat pointed to the floating craft, which had started to fly away above the treetops.

"There," he said.

"That?"

The Rat nodded. "How do you think the King would feel if we were to give him that, and all the fleshy deliciousness that scurries upon it?"

The Other Rat Creature thought carefully, chewing on a claw. "I think he might be very happy."

"Exactly," the Rat said. "And if he's happy, he won't want to kill us anymore."

The Other smiled, showing off rows of sharp yellow teeth. "Yes, I think you're right."

"And in his overwhelming gratitude," the Rat added, "he would allow us to keep Fredrick." The Rat hugged his decaying prize, swaying from side to side. "And all our problems will be solved."

His friend thought some more as he watched the object growing smaller in the distance.

"So how do we capture it?" he asked.

The Rat stopped hugging his squirrel for a moment. "Must I think of everything?" he snapped. "I've already come up with the plan. Don't you think it's your turn to come up with how we execute it?"

The Other Rat gulped in fear. "Execute? Don't use that word," he warned, fearful of their fate if King Agak were to find them before they could acquire this special gift.

The sky wagon would soon be out of sight. He had to come up with something . . . anything.

"I say we follow it and wait for an opportunity to pounce," he declared.

The Rat Creature was silent, continuing to pat the gray fur of the dead rodent. "Pouncing is good," he finally said with a nod.

And without another word, the pair slunk quickly through the forest, their eyes locked upon the strange craft that floated through the sky.

Waiting for their opportunity.

• • •

From behind the locked door of his cell, Randolf watched the three deputies and the Constable. They moved as if they weren't used to their bodies, as if they were no longer in possession of themselves, as if something else — something dark — had taken control.

"Would you look at these," the thing wearing the body of Constable Roarke said. The man was flexing the fingers of his large hands, looking at them as if seeing them for the first time.

Randolf noticed that even his voice sounded different.

"This is much nicer than rotting animal flesh, isn't it, boys?"

The deputies laughed maniacally. They, too, were checking out the movement of their new limbs.

"Much nicer," one of them agreed. "I could get used to this."

The Constable chuckled, and it sounded like he was getting ready to cough something up.

"When the Nacht takes over this place, perhaps he will reward us with these bodies."

Hearing the chilling words, Randolf's fears were confirmed. The four men were indeed possessed by something not of this world. Something that had somehow found its way into the world from the Dreaming.

The Constable suddenly noticed Randolf and examined him with eyes of liquid black.

"Hello there, holy man," he croaked.

Randolf tensed.

"Is he the one?" a deputy asked.

The Constable nodded, a malicious grin spreading across his face.

"What are we to do with him?" another of the deputies questioned, rubbing his hands together in anticipation.

"We are to prevent the Veni Yan from interfering with our master's plans," the Constable said.

"How do we do that?" a third deputy inquired.

"Yeah, how do we stop him?" echoed one of the others.

"Why, the worst ways we can think of, of course," the Constable said as he lurched forward. He reached out to grab the prisoner but was stopped by the metal bars of the cell door. Randolf pressed himself against the opposite wall as the Constable furiously shook the bars.

"Open this door," the Constable commanded him.

"I'm sorry," Randolf said. "Even if I could, I seriously doubt I would."

The Constable let out a low growl before turning to the others.

"Don't just stand there. Help me!"

The others stumbled toward their commander, trying out their new legs. They stopped just before the cell door, inspecting the bars with their black, shiny eyes.

"We need to get this open," one of the deputies said.

"You don't say," the Constable said with a scowl. "Of course we need to get it open . . . but how? It's locked."

Randolf watched as the possessed paced back and forth in front of the cell. He could tell they were thinking, trying to figure out how they could get at him.

"A key!" one of the deputies suddenly exclaimed.

"Yes, excellent," Constable Roarke approved. He held out his hand. "Give it to me."

The deputy looked at his leader sheepishly. "I don't know where it is," he said, shrugging his shoulders.

Randolf was grateful that the possessed creatures did not appear to have access to their captors' memories. He distinctly remembered watching Constable Roarke place his heavy, metal key ring in a large wooden box on a lower shelf of the table across the room.

The Constable's face screwed up in fury as he looked through the bars at Randolf. "Do you know where the key is, Veni Yan?"

Randolf answered with a silent shrug of his shoulders.

"Very well," the Constable said softly. "We could have made your fate swift and only momentarily painful, but now you have angered me beyond mercy."

Randolf chose to remain silent, sitting on the mattress stuffed with straw at the back of his cell.

"Remember, we gave you a chance," the Constable

snarled. He looked to his deputies. "If the men whose bodies we now control locked this one in there," he said, pointing through the bars at Randolf, "then the key is here somewhere." He motioned with his large hand around the room. "Find it," he barked.

The possessed lurched into action, and the Constable turned back to Randolf. He stepped very close to the cell door, peering in at him from between the bars.

"We'll be with you in just a minute."

Percival thought he might just want to have his head examined. Hands clutching the *Queen of the Sky*'s wheel, he steered the craft through the clouds on a rescue mission he knew very little about and that could very well place him, as well as his niece and nephew, smack-dab in the middle of danger.

Yep, head-examining time.

But there was something about the kid, this Tom Elm, that made Percival want to trust him, and if what the kid had explained was true, the whole Valley and beyond could be in a world of trouble if somebody didn't do something about it.

"Dang it," Percival muttered in frustration, giving the wheel a violent shake. He hated when he got himself into situations like this. He was all for the thrill of adventure, but risking his and the twins' lives was another story.

"Is there a problem, Percival Bone?" a creepy woman's voice asked from somewhere in the cramped space of the wheelhouse.

"Who's that?" Percival asked, head whipping around, but he saw no one.

"It is I," said the voice.

It was coming from somewhere right in front of him.

"Where . . . ?" he began, but then he saw it.

Saw *her*.

"EEEEK!" the Bone explorer shrieked, jumping back from the ship's wheel. "What're you doing there?"

Looking at him from the center of the wheel was the face of the plant woman . . . the face of Lorimar.

"I must remain connected to organic life in some way if I am to travel," she began to explain. "So I have inhabited your sky ship."

"Inhabited?" Percival questioned. "You're living in the *Queen*?"

"Yes, Percival Bone, I'm living inside the wood of your craft."

"Now I've seen everything," the Bone said, but deep down he knew that wasn't true. There were still more fantastic things to come — of that, he was certain.

He stepped back up to the wheel and took hold of it.

"Is everything all right?" Lorimar asked from its center.

"Fine," Percival said, eyes darting from the window before him, to the face in the wheel, and then back again. "You startled me is all."

"Are you certain that is all?" she asked.

"Yeah, I'm just ducky," the Bone explorer said with more sarcasm than he intended. He reached up and fiddled distractedly with the valves of the ship.

"What are your concerns?" Lorimar asked.

He was going to bite his tongue and keep it all to himself, but he couldn't help it. His daddy had always said the best way to deal with a problem was to never let it become one, so Percival decided to speak his mind.

"The biggest one is how I managed to get myself into this fix," he said, looking down at the center of the wheel.

"But you agreed to help us —" she began.

"Yeah, and I'm beginning to think I spoke too soon."

"You were chosen as well," Lorimar added.

"You keep saying that, but chosen by who? I don't get it," Percival grumbled as he looked out at the open sky.

"The Dreaming has chosen you . . . the Dreaming has chosen you all as champions against the Nacht," Lorimar explained.

"And this guy we're going to rescue? He's been chosen, too?"

"Yes," she confirmed. "The Dreaming has chosen each of you for a special reason. The Dreaming does not make mistakes."

Hmmm, Percival thought. "So this Nacht . . . he's pretty powerful?"

"That is an understatement," Lorimar answered. "If not stopped, the Nacht will threaten the very existence of two worlds — the Dreaming and the Waking World."

Percival was silent for a moment, thinking about the path of the unknown before him. He had no problem with a little danger every now and then; in fact, he kind of thrived on it. But now he had Abbey and Barclay to consider.

"I'm afraid for the kids," he said finally. He glanced out onto the deck, at Abbey and Barclay showing off the ship to Tom and the raccoon, Roderick.

"I'd like to keep them out of harm's way if I can," he said. The pained expression on Lorimar's face let Percival know he wasn't going to like what she was about to say next.

"With the threat of the Nacht all around us, Percival Bone," she warned, "it is too late for that. They are already in harm's way."

Percival sighed and took one more look at his niece and nephew before turning back to piloting the *Queen*.

"That's what I was afraid of."

Chapter 11

The possessed men continued to tear the jailhouse apart, growling and carrying on like animals as they searched for the key to the cell.

Randolf gave them nothing. He simply sat on his mattress, trying to will them away from the box that contained their prize.

"He knows where it is," one of the deputies said as he tore open a cabinet that housed swords and other weapons. "Just look at him sitting there all smug."

"Don't worry about him," Constable Roarke ordered. "It's only a matter of time before we find the key, and then we'll see how smug he is."

The deputy laughed. It was a chilling sound, but Randolf acted as though he didn't hear it. He had to remain calm, to prepare himself in case an opportunity presented itself. Self-control under pressure was one of the first things he had learned as a Veni Yan warrior, and it had saved his life on many an occasion.

But it hadn't been able to save his wife and child.

The Constable suddenly looked at him intently and tilted his head back, sniffing the air.

"What's that smell?" he asked, making his way closer to the cell. "Is that the delicious aroma of failure and regret tinged with sorrow?"

Somehow the creature could smell Randolf's emotions, and it drew closer to the bars of the cell, like a wolf to the scent of blood.

"So much sadness," the Constable observed as he peered through the bars. "Perhaps that is why the Nacht is so desperate for us to take care of you."

The Nacht, Randolf thought. *That must be their master.*

"You know what they say about those whose hearts are filled with regret and sorrow . . . they have nothing to lose, and that makes them dangerous."

Randolf said nothing, and the monsters continued to rip the room apart, one of them dangerously close to the box that held the keys.

"You're not dangerous, are you, priest?" the Constable growled.

Suddenly, there was an ear-piercing shriek of triumph, and Randolf looked past the Constable to see that one of the deputies was dancing around, keys jingling in his hand. The others howled and cried out with pleasure before they all joined their leader at the door to Randolf's cell.

"Stop that nonsense and give them to me!" Roarke barked. They all went silent, and the deputy with the keys handed them over.

"It is time, Veni Yan." The Constable jangled the keys sinisterly before trying the first of them in the lock. "As soon as we find the right one . . ."

The possessed began to cackle, eager to get their hands on him.

Randolf was anxious as well, waiting for an opening. He ignored their laughter, listening to the sound of each key as it was placed into the lock.

One after another.

Metal on metal.

Randolf waited, waited for the sound.

Click!

The Veni Yan tensed in anticipation as the door was unlocked and pulled open. He sprang up from the bed and threw himself at his enemies, the Constable's last question of him echoing in his ear.

You're not dangerous, are you, priest?

Randolf would give the Constable his answer.

He would show him how dangerous he could be.

• • •

The *Queen of the Sky* came to a gradual stop over a sheep pasture. From the ship's deck, Tom could see Trumble not far off in the distance. He felt a nervous twist in his belly and again wondered how it was possible that he, the son of a turnip farmer, had ended up here and now. He'd already pinched and poked himself a hundred times, but he wasn't dreaming. Everything that was happening was real, as crazy as it all was. He sure hoped the Dreaming knew what it was doing.

"All right, then," he heard Percival say.

Tom turned to find the Bone explorer coming from the wheelhouse with a grim expression.

"Lorimar says that the air is pretty thick with danger, so we're gonna need to shake a leg if —"

"Lorimar says?" Tom asked.

"Yeah, I was just talking to her in the wheelhouse," Percival replied, hooking a thumb toward the small room behind him.

For a second, Tom thought he was making some kind of weird joke but then realized that Percival was serious. He went to the wheelhouse and took a quick peek inside, finding no one.

"Percival, there's no one in there," he said, trying not to sound rude. "Lorimar didn't come with us . . . remember?"

Roderick and the twins had come to join them.

"What's going on?" Roderick asked.

Percival smiled slyly. "Tom here thinks that I might've misplaced a few of my marbles," he said, tapping the side of his head with a thick finger.

The raccoon gasped and began to look around the deck. "Do you want us to help you find them?"

Percival laughed. "No, that's okay, Roderick. I just need to explain something to Tom here."

Tom was really confused now.

"We thought that Lorimar didn't come with us," the Bone said slowly, "but she really did."

Tom looked around. And then he heard it, an odd popping and cracking, like the sound trees make when bent by heavy winds.

"Hello, Tom," a familiar voice said.

"There she is." Percival pointed to a spot behind where Tom was standing.

"Where who is?" Abbey asked.

"Yeah, who're we talking about? Did they take your marbles?" Barclay wanted to know.

Tom turned around, at first seeing nothing but the wooden side of the ship and the open sky beyond it.

"I'm here, Tom," the voice said.

And finally, Tom saw it . . . saw *her*.

Lorimar's face had appeared in the side of the *Queen*, and she was staring at him. Tom jumped back with a yelp.

"That's her . . . that's Lorimar!" he exclaimed in surprise.

"Wow, look at that," Roderick said, as both he and the twins approached the face of wood.

"How'd she get in there?" Abbey wanted to know . . . and so did Tom.

"I guess it's the only way she can travel," Percival attempted to explain. "She has to stay connected to the elements."

Tom looked from Lorimar's face to the Bone. "So she's *inside* the wood of the ship?" he asked, not quite believing what he was seeing.

Roderick and the twins huddled around Lorimar's face, reaching out with careful fingers to gently touch it.

"My spirit inhabits things of the earth . . . what lives, or as in the case of this sky vessel, what was once alive."

Tom was relieved. "I'm glad you're still with us," he said to the face in the side of the ship. "I wasn't sure we could do this without you."

Her eyes shifted with a slight creak to look at him. "Of course you could have," Lorimar said very seriously. "The Dreaming would never have chosen someone who was incapable."

That made Tom feel good, but he still wasn't sure. It was great to know that the Dreaming had confidence in him, but did he actually believe it himself?

Percival clapped his hands, drawing their attention.

"All right, then, now that we got that business out of

the way," he said. "I believe we've got somebody waiting for a rescue."

"That's right," Tom said, stepping forward. "The priest is in Trumble." Tom pointed over the side. "On the other side of those trees."

"We'll leave the *Queen* here, then," Percival Bone said, going to the side of the sky ship and looking down. "This sheep field should do us quite nicely."

"Drop anchor, Uncle Percy?" Barclay asked, moving toward where it lay atop a pile of coiled rope. His sister quickly intercepted him, knocking him from his path.

"You dropped anchor last time," she said. "And besides, the oldest always gets to drop anchor."

"Who says?" Barclay objected, hands on his hips.

"It's a law," Abbey said with confidence.

"What law?" Barclay asked. "I've never heard of such a thing."

"That's because you're not the oldest," she said, and bent down to pick up the anchor with a grunt.

Tom could see that she was having some difficulty but knew she would never ask for help. Abbey reminded him quite a bit of his little sister, Lottie, and he felt a pang in his gut as he watched her.

"Here, let me help you with that," he offered.

A spark of anger flashed in her eyes, and for a moment, Tom thought she was going to yell at him as she'd been endlessly yelling at her brother. But the fire quickly went out and she smiled instead.

"Thanks, Tom," she said, and quickly looked away, hiding her grin. They shuffled over to the side of the ship and hauled the anchor up and over.

"Why didn't she punch him?" Barclay asked Roderick, who stood beside him, watching.

The raccoon shrugged. "I don't know. Tom's a nice guy."

"I'm a nice guy," Barclay responded. "She eats nice guys for breakfast."

Tom glanced over at Lorimar's face. Her eyes were tightly closed.

"Are you all right, Lorimar?" Tom asked.

"The Nacht," she said, eyes opening with a soft creak. "His presence is growing stronger in the Waking World."

And before he could ask what they should do, Percival was already on the move.

"Then it sounds like we don't have time to waste," the Bone said. He turned and marched back into the wheelhouse, taking the stairs below deck.

They all waited in silence until the adventurer returned, carrying something that Tom had never seen before.

"We're gonna need this," Percival said, holding up the long object that appeared to be made of metal and wood. It had a strange funnel at the end. Tom couldn't even begin to guess what it was used for.

"What is it?" Roderick asked before Tom could.

"This is Susie," Percival said proudly. "She's my blunderbuss."

"You know it's for real when Uncle Percy breaks out Susie," Barclay said with a smile. "Nobody messes with Susie."

"What's a blunderbuss?" Tom felt a little stupid for asking, but he guessed he wasn't the only one who didn't understand.

"Susie is our way of defending ourselves," Percival explained. "When something bad gets in our faces, Susie tells it to get out of the way."

"It talks?" Roderick asked.

"In a manner of speaking," Percival answered. "She has quite the loud voice when she's making her point."

"Hello, Susie," the raccoon said with a little wave.

Tom still didn't understand what Susie was all about, but he felt a little bit safer knowing that she would be going with them.

"So who's going into town?" Percival asked, slinging the weapon over his shoulder.

"Me!" Abbey shrieked, standing on the tips of her toes.

"Me, too!" Barclay said right after.

"No, it might be dangerous," the twins' uncle told them with a shake of his head, and their faces fell.

"But we eat danger for breakfast," Barclay said, throwing his hands into the air.

"Not today, you don't," Percival answered. "Consider yourselves on a danger diet."

"And besides," Tom piped up, not wanting the twins to feel left out, "we're going to need somebody to stay here and watch the ship. . . . Isn't that right, Percival?"

The Bone adventurer caught on. "Yes, that's true," he said. "We're going to need the bravest of the brave to stay right here and watch the *Queen* so nobody takes her while we're in the village."

"We can do that!" the twins cried in unison.

"And me, too!" Roderick added, throwing a furry arm into the air.

"You, too, Roderick," Tom told his little friend.

"Time is of the essence," Lorimar said. "We must leave at once."

Tom was about to ask her if she would be coming with them, but she had disappeared. He reached out and touched the smooth surface of the wood and found no trace of the woman's face.

"C'mon, Tom, no time like the here and now," Percival agreed, putting Susie's leather strap over his shoulder before grabbing hold of the rope ladder and tossing it over the side. "The quicker we find the newest member of our little party, the quicker we can get on with our quest."

"Be good, Roderick." The raccoon waved as the boy climbed over the side, followed by Percival.

"Good luck, Uncle Percy!" Barclay called out.

"Be safe!" Abbey added.

"You two kids be good, now," Percival said as he went down the ladder. "And don't touch anything."

Once on the ground, Tom looked around. He was about to say something about Lorimar when suddenly the earth began to churn, and a figure made of roots, dirt, leaves, and rock sprang up before them.

"I was wondering if you were going to join us," Tom said with a smile.

Lorimar bowed ever so slightly.

"All right, then," Percival said. "Now that we're all present and accounted for, let's get rambling." The Bone adventurer turned and started in the direction of the village.

"They'll be fine, won't they?" Tom asked, following with Lorimar. He turned around to see Abbey, Barclay, and Roderick waving furiously. "How much trouble could they possibly get into?"

They were all silent for a moment.

"Like I said before," Percival finally replied, "let's get back as quick as we can."

"There it is," the Rat Creature gasped, fanning his overheated face with the body of his dead squirrel, Fredrick. "It's stopped."

The Other Rat joined his friend behind the cover of an oak tree and carefully peeked out at the object floating over the open field.

"Now's our chance," he said with a growl, his thick tongue running over his pointed teeth.

"Can't we just rest a bit?" the Rat Creature asked, still fanning himself. "I'm exhausted after all that running."

"But it's right there," the Other pointed out. "Just floating and waiting to be pounced upon."

"Oh yes, the pouncing," the tired Rat said between gulps of air. "I really do need a minute if I'm going to pounce."

His comrade crossed his furry arms and stared at him intently. "A minute, that's all. Then we attack."

The Rat agreed, dropping his shaggy butt to the forest floor and leaning back against the tree. "Do you think Freddy and I have time for a power nap?"

The Other just rolled his eyes.

"It's awfully quiet," Tom said as they entered the village.

There wasn't a soul around, even though it was late morning, when the shops and market should have been bustling.

"Look at that," Percival said, pointing to one of the farm stands.

A man and a woman, who reminded Tom of his parents, were fast asleep, curled up in tight balls on the ground beside a wheelbarrow filled with onions. They were moaning and twitching, as if in the grip of a nightmare.

"Did the Nacht do this?" Tom asked Lorimar, but he already knew the answer.

"The Nacht was here." The forest woman gazed around at their surroundings, long, sinewy roots snaking out from her body and swaying in the breeze.

"Is he still around?" Percival asked nervously, and he clutched Susie all the tighter.

Lorimar did not answer at first. The roots grew longer, their squirming reminding Tom of the worms that wiggled from the ground after a heavy rain.

"Yes, his presence still taints the air," she finally said. She raised an arm and pointed past the marketplace. "There," she said, almost in a trance. "The Nacht's evil can still be found there."

"That's probably where we need to go, then," Tom said after only a moment's hesitation. He had no idea when he'd become so brave, but it just felt like the right thing to do. Scary, but still the right thing.

As they walked, they continued to see signs of the Nacht's influence; people had dropped where they stood and were lying on the ground, unnaturally asleep.

"They're going to be okay, right?" he asked Lorimar.

"I do not know," the tree woman answered. "Our quest has only just begun."

"Great," Percival muttered under his breath. "Don't put too much pressure on us now."

Tom knew exactly how the Bone felt. He was still trying to understand why the Dreaming would choose him to be its champion. The whole thing was crazy.

But right now, they had to rescue the warrior priest, and who were they to argue with the Dreaming anyway?

Every noise, no matter how soft, was startling in the silence of the sleeping village — every creak of a window shutter, or cry of a bird — and they jumped at every sound.

"You said that in your vision this priest fella was locked in a cell?" Percival asked.

"Yes," Tom answered. "So we must be looking for the village jail."

As they neared a squat stone building, they heard the muffled sound of thumps and bangs, followed by an unearthly squeal.

"Something tells me we've found the place we're looking for," Percival said. A hand-painted sign that read CONSTABLE'S OFFICE hung on a chain above the heavy, wooden door.

The closer they got, the louder the scuffling became. Tom took the lead, carefully approaching the door. From the sounds of it, there was a tremendous battle going on inside.

"The evil is here," Lorimar said, glaring at the door.

"Should I knock first?" Tom asked, turning to his companions.

"Let me do it." Percival quickly walked up alongside the boy. "Knock, knock," he said as he lifted a foot and kicked the door as hard as he could.

The door flew open and crashed off the wall, and they all charged in.

The room was in shambles, furniture overturned, some smashed into kindling. Five men were in the midst of a struggle in the center of the room. It appeared to be four against one, and as Tom looked closer, he recognized the Veni Yan priest in the center of the fight.

The older man was doing a fine job throwing kicks and punches and sending his attackers flying, but they always came back at him, no matter how hard they were hit.

And then Tom heard them speak.

"Give up, priest," said one in a voice that was all too familiar.

"It'll only hurt for a moment or so," growled another, conjuring images in the boy's mind of dead animals crawling from the darkness of the forest around his parents' home.

"We have to help him," Tom whispered to himself, and then louder so his friends could hear. "We have to help him."

Percival nodded, aiming Susie at the ceiling.

"First we gotta get their attention."

The Bone flexed his finger on the trigger of the weapon, and Tom cringed as the blunderbuss roared, the explosion from its funneled end putting a hole in the ceiling.

The deafening blast had the desired effect.

"It's the boy!" one of the men said, and they all stopped and turned their shiny, black eyes to the intruders.

"I was hoping we'd get another crack at him," said another.

"I'll deal with the old man," said the largest of the men, with a curling mustache. "You three take care of the boy and his friends."

"Okay," Tom said. "Looks like we got their attention . . . now what?"

The priest had been driven to the floor, and slowly he raised his head. His soft, brown eyes met Tom's, and the boy instantly felt a connection. This was the man who was supposed to be with them.

"Run," the man said as he scrambled to his feet. "Run for your lives!"

They heard the sound of the door slam behind them and all turned to see one of the possessed men grinning from ear to ear and sticking to the closed door like a giant spider.

"You're not going anywhere," he growled, eyes glistening wetly. "The Nacht has plans for all of you."

"Hey, you're not supposed to be eating those," Barclay said to Roderick. The raccoon had found an open crate of potatoes and had helped himself.

"Why not?" he asked between chews.

"Because that's how we power the *Queen*'s engines," the little Bone explained. "If you eat all the potatoes, we won't be able to make the propellers on the engine spin, or make our lights light."

Roderick stared at the half-eaten potato. "Can I at least finish this one?" he asked. "I'm starved."

As if on cue, Barclay's stomach rumbled noisily.

"Yeah, I'm pretty hungry, too."

The raccoon held out the potato to him. "Bite?"

The boy thought for a second before taking it.

"Sure," he said. "And after this, we'll go down into the supply room to see if there's any crackers."

"I love crackers," Roderick said before taking the potato back.

Abbey came around the wheelhouse with a broom and was sweeping the deck, when she noticed them.

"Hey, what are you two doing?" she asked, dropping the broom and angrily stomping over to them.

"Nothing," Barclay answered.

"Nawfin," Roderick said through a mouthful of potato.

"Is that a potato you're eating?" she asked, pointing at what little was left in Roderick's paw. "Uncle Percival is gonna be really angry if he finds out you've been eating the ship's power source."

"I already explained it to him," Barclay said, defending his new friend. "He won't be eating any more. In fact, we were just gonna go and get some crackers. . . . C'mon, Roderick."

The two started to leave, but Abbey blocked their way.

"You two aren't going anywhere," she said with authority. "You've got chores to do."

"Chores!" Roderick and Barclay exclaimed in unison.

"Yep." Abbey retrieved the broom from the deck and handed it to her brother. "Uncle Percy left me in charge, and I say you've got chores to do."

Barclay refused to take the broom.

"He did not leave you in charge," the boy yelled. "If he was gonna leave anybody in charge, it would have been me."

"He would not!" Abbey shrieked. "I'm the oldest and I'm in charge."

"But you don't know how to fly the *Queen of the Sky* and I do."

"I do so know how to fly the *Queen of the Sky*," Abbey protested.

"Oh yeah?" Barclay said. "Well, if you're so smart, show me."

His sister spun around and stalked across the deck. Barclay and Roderick followed closely at her heels.

"Uncle Percy showed me how to fly the *Queen* lots of times," Abbey said as she entered the wheelhouse.

"He did not," Barclay insisted. "You were always too busy playing with your stupid dolls and having tea parties."

"Shows how much you know. Uncle Percy used to come to my tea parties, and after tea he would show me and my dolls how to fly the *Queen of the Sky*."

"You're such a liar!" Barclay yelled.

"Am not!" Abbey screamed back.

"Then show me!" Barclay ordered. "Since you're so smart, show me how to make the *Queen* fly."

Abbey turned to the controls.

"Ummm, guys?" Roderick interjected. "I don't remember who Percival left in charge, but I do remember him telling us not to touch anything."

Barclay looked at the raccoon with a smirk.

"Don't worry, Roderick," he said. "She doesn't know the first thing about flying this ship."

Abbey stepped closer to the *Queen*'s control center and

looked down at all the knobs and gauges. She reached out but then hesitated, her fingers hovering over some buttons and shiny switches.

"See, told ya, you don't know how," Barclay taunted.

And that, apparently, was all she needed.

Abbey reached down and began to flip the switches, and the lights on the *Queen*'s control panel turned to red. She grabbed hold of the knobs and gave each of them a sharp turn to the right.

A tremble went through the body of the hovering sky craft, and Abbey, Barclay, and Roderick stumbled back as the *Queen of the Sky* began to float upward.

"See?" Abbey said proudly. "Told ya I could make her fly."

"All right, all right, make her stop," Barclay said, suddenly nervous.

A look of concern came over his sister's face.

"What is it?" Barclay asked. "What's wrong?"

"I don't know how to stop it," she said, panic creeping into her voice.

"What do you mean you don't know how to stop it?!" Barclay exclaimed. "I thought you knew how to fly this thing!"

"I thought *you* knew how to fly this thing!" Abbey cried.

"Since when do you believe anything I have to say?"

Barclay responded, jumping up and down in front of the fully lit instrument panel.

Roderick squeezed in between the panicking twins.

"We've got to do something," he said, climbing up onto the edge of the ship's control panel. "What about that button?"

"This one?" Abbey asked. Roderick nodded, and she pushed it.

The ship shuddered again, and they heard a loud hiss. The *Queen* began to rise faster.

"What'd you do that for?" Barclay cried. "Now we're gonna keep going up until we get to the moon . . . and I don't wanna go to the moon!" He looked above their heads at the series of knobs, reached up, and gave the middle one a good turn. Again there was an enormous, snakelike hiss, and they could feel the *Queen of the Sky* begin to descend.

"Now all we gotta do is turn off the engines," Barclay said, pushing his sister out of the way with his hip. Abbey didn't care for that in the least and she tackled him, their struggles knocking Roderick onto the ship's controls.

"Watch it, you two!" he screeched.

The raccoon tried not to touch anything, but he accidentally pushed some buttons and flipped a switch or two with his feet as he tried to stand. And as Abbey and Barclay continued to fight, pushing and slapping at

each other, the *Queen of the Sky* glided forward at an ever-increasing speed.

Piloted by no one.

"It's leaving!" the Rat Creature shrieked, frantically waving the dead squirrel clutched in his clawed hand.

"But look," the Other Rat said. "It has a tail."

They watched as the floating craft first began to drift upward, and then forward, dragging behind it a length of rope with a large, hooked piece of metal at its end.

"We can use that to capture it," the Rat Creature said, tapping Fredrick's head on the palm of his hand. "And then we can turn it over to the King, and our problems will be solved."

"Yes," the Other hissed, eyes still fixed upon the craft drifting in the sky. "But there won't be any problems solved if we allow it to escape."

"Quickly," the Rat Creature said, bounding from their hiding place. "We can't let our prize get away."

The Other Rat followed, watching as the *Queen*'s anchor dragged across the ground, digging up the grass of the sheep field.

"Grab it!" the Rat Creature wailed. "I've only got one hand!"

"Then drop the squirrel!" the Other retorted.

"I'll do no such thing; Fredrick and I are meant to be together."

The sky ship began to fly higher, wobbling a bit from the anchor's weight.

"It's getting away!" the Rat Creature squealed.

"Not from me, it isn't," the Other growled, tensing his legs and springing upward. He grabbed hold of the anchor and held on with all his might. "Got you!" he cried victoriously.

"It's not stopping!" the Rat Creature shouted, frantically trying to keep up with his friend, who was now being lifted into the air.

The Other reached down. "Quickly, take my paw!"

The Rat Creature gently placed Fredrick in his mouth, and then jumped, grabbing hold of his comrade's outstretched arm with both hands.

Within seconds they were both very high above the ground, hanging on for dear life.

"This didn't turn out quite like I expected," the Rat Creature said.

"Sometimes we're so stupid I'm amazed that we've survived this long," said the Other with disgust.

CHAPTER 1.2

Tom didn't think he'd ever been so terrified.

The men with darkness for eyes began to circle them. Their skin was incredibly pale, as if all color had somehow been sucked away, and the way they moved — stiff and jerky — just wasn't natural. Neither was the fact that they seemed to be able to climb the walls like oversized bugs.

The Veni Yan priest stood with Tom and his companions as the monsters — he couldn't call them men anymore — glared menacingly at them. The priest looked tired, and the haggard lines under his eyes showed age. He wasn't the kind of person Tom thought would be on his quest, but then again, neither was he or the others the Dreaming had chosen, so what did he know?

"Why are you here, boy?" the priest asked, his gaze locked upon the threat circling closer to them.

"We came to rescue you," Tom said, trying to keep his voice steady and strong.

"Rescue me?" the priest questioned with a sarcastic laugh. "Why would you want to do a foolish thing like that?"

"Because the Dreaming told me to."

The priest studied the boy. "The Dreaming, you say?"

Tom was about to answer when the leader of the monsters, the one who wore the Constable's badge, spoke.

"You can't trust the Dreaming, Tom," the Constable said with an evil grin. "Look at all the trouble it's brought you."

"We warned you, Tom," a deputy said from where he stuck to the wall. "First your family and now this entire village are suffering because of you."

The words stung.

"Don't listen to them, Tom," Lorimar said, placing a rough hand of bark on his shoulder. "It is their job to plant the seeds of doubt in your mind."

"Oh yes, this is all your fault. If you had done what we asked and stopped all this quest foolishness, things wouldn't be so bad," chimed in another.

"And now we're going to make you all wish you'd never come," threatened a third.

The monsters moved closer, the one stuck to the wall springing to the floor to join his brethren. Tom knew there wasn't much time.

"This is what happens when you don't listen to your elders," the Constable said as, one by one, each of the monsters drew their swords.

"Doesn't Susie have something to say right about now?" Tom nervously asked Percival.

"Well, it's kinda embarrassing," the Bone said, frantically fishing through the multiple pockets of his shirt. "But I'm outta shot. Looks like I only brought enough for one blast."

"One blast?" Tom asked in disbelief. "What good is a weapon you can only use once?"

The Bone shrugged. "Usually, once is all you need."

"Lorimar?" Tom asked. "Any ideas?"

"Stand close to me," the tree woman suddenly ordered.

The monsters reacted to her voice.

"Do not involve yourself in this, spirit," the Constable warned her. "You are already in enough trouble."

Ignoring him, she extended her twiglike fingers toward the floor. She closed her eyes, and her mossy lips began to move silently.

The monsters charged, their weapons raised to strike, when the floor started to violently tremble. Tom gasped as he realized something was moving beneath the wooden floors.

"Stay close," Lorimar warned them again. The floorboards creaked and moaned as something pushed from beneath, snapping the thick boards with its force.

Tom couldn't believe his eyes as he watched a tree grow up from the floor into the room, its boughs becoming thick with dark green leaves as it matured before their eyes. The tree grew higher and higher, until its branches pressed tight against the jail's ceiling, until it punched its way through the roof out into the freedom of daylight.

"Would you look at that," Percival said in awe, tilting his head back to admire the awesome sight. Even the monsters appeared stunned.

"Climb," the forest woman instructed.

"You don't have to tell me twice," Percival Bone said. He grabbed hold of one of the lower branches and hauled himself up into the body of the tree.

And then the monsters realized what they were doing.

"Stop them!" the Constable roared.

The monsters made toward the tree, but Lorimar was not yet done.

She waved her arms, and thick, powerful branches erupted from the tree's trunk, placing a barrier between the monsters and them.

"Quickly now," she urged.

Tom gripped the Veni Yan's arm and pulled him toward the tree. "Can you climb?" he asked.

The older man smiled. "It's been many years, but I doubt I've forgotten."

Tom was surprised at the old-timer's agility as he followed Percival up the tree toward the hole in the jail's ceiling.

"C'mon, Lorimar, you're next," Tom said to the forest woman.

"Have no concerns about me," she said, gesturing for him to climb. He was about to argue when her body fell apart again — leaves, dirt, rocks, and vines dropping to the floor. Tom didn't have time to wonder where she'd gone. He pulled himself into the tree as the monsters used their swords to hack through the thick branches that blocked their way.

Glancing down as he climbed, Tom saw that two of the monsters had already broken through and were starting up the tree after them. Tom's thoughts raced. *Where'll we go once we get to the roof? We can't hold off the Nacht's soldiers much longer.* He climbed out of the jagged hole in the ceiling onto the flat roof of the jail, wishing as hard as he could for a miracle.

"Where's the tree lady?" Percival asked.

"She did that thing she does again," Tom said. "Told me not to worry about her and fell to pieces."

"I wish I could do that right about now," Percival said as the first of the monsters emerged from the hole.

"There's no escaping us," it cackled.

"No harm in trying, though," Percival said, hurrying over to where the monster's head poked out.

"Could you give me a hand?" he had the nerve to ask, reaching toward Percival for assistance.

"No problem," the Bone replied. He unslung Susie from his shoulder, and using it like a club, struck his enemy over the head. The monster cried out in pain and tumbled backward, knocking the other of the Nacht's men from their perch.

"That should buy us a little time," Percival said, returning Susie to her place over his shoulder.

"Time for what?" the Veni Yan priest asked. "We only delay the inevitable." He was standing at the edge of the roof, looking out over the town.

The Constable's bellows of rage floated up from below, and Tom looked through the hole to see that the two monsters were already on their way back up.

"Think!" he said. "There has to be a way out. The Dreaming wouldn't have trusted us with a mission this important if we couldn't figure out how to get out of messes like this."

Percival began to pace. "Kid's got a point," he said. The Bone stroked his chin as he walked back and forth. "Think, Percival, think."

"Think fast, we're running low on time," Tom urged.

"There is no answer," the Veni Yan said, throwing up his hands. "We're not about to grow wings and fly away!"

Tom didn't want to agree with the old man, but he was

frustrated and very close to giving up. That's when he saw it. At first he thought it was a bird — a really large bird — but then it got closer. This was the answer to their pleas.

The *Queen of the Sky* was sailing through the air toward them.

"Nope, we certainly can't grow wings," Tom agreed. "But how about the next best thing?"

He could tell that the warrior priest was confused, and just as Percival was about to ask what he was talking about, Tom pointed.

"Would you look at that!" the Bone adventurer exclaimed, doing a little dance. "I'm not gonna even ask how it's possible; that would just be rude."

Tom and Percival ran to the building's edge as the Veni Yan priest turned to see what had gotten their attention.

"By the Red Dragon's beard, what is it?" he asked in awe.

"That's our ticket to freedom," Percival said, waving at the approaching craft.

Tom started to wave but became distracted by the sight of the anchor that still hung beneath the sky vessel, and what desperately clung to it.

"What's that?" Tom asked.

"What's what?" Percival asked.

"That, hanging from the anchor."

The Bone squinted as the ship glided closer. "Well, I'll be plucked and breaded," he said.

"Hairy Men," the Veni Yan priest snarled.

"How the heck did they get there?" Percival asked.

Tom had no idea. How was it possible that two Rat Creatures were hanging from the *Queen of the Sky*'s anchor?

And did Abbey, Barclay, and Roderick know about it?

Roderick scampered across the wooden deck of the ship and hopped up onto the bow.

"I can see Trumble!" He turned his head and yelled to his friends in the wheelhouse. "It's right up ahead!"

Abbey poked her head out and gave him a thumbs-up.

It seemed that the twins were actually getting the hang of flying the sky ship, and all it took was for them to stop yelling and hitting each other for five seconds.

Roderick looked out over the little village below, surprised that he didn't see any people moving about. *Curious*, the raccoon thought, but he was soon distracted by thoughts of all the different kinds of food he could find in the market he caught sight of below.

Gurgle, his stomach said.

He'd never gotten any of those crackers that Barclay promised, and then he remembered the potatoes. One more might make him feel better.

After checking to make sure that the twins weren't watching, Roderick jumped down to the deck and dashed over to the open box of potatoes. He quietly lifted the lid, picked out a big round one, and ran back to his perch at the front of the ship. He brushed some of the dirt from the vegetable and then took a good-sized bite.

As he chewed, he saw movement not too far off in the distance. Three figures were standing on the roof of a building with a tree growing out of it. *That's sort of strange*, the raccoon thought, trying to remember the last time he'd seen a tree growing like that.

One of the figures was waving at him, jumping up and down, and Roderick happily waved back. *They seem very friendly in this village*, he thought, taking another bite from his snack.

As the ship floated closer, he could make out a boy, an older man, and a Bone. *What a coincidence*, the raccoon thought, happily gnawing on his potato. *Wait until Tom and Percival hear about this.*

"Hey, wait a second, that *is* Tom and Percival!" the little raccoon suddenly exclaimed, waving all the harder. "Hey, guys, it's us!"

"What are you yelling for?" Abbey asked, darting from the wheelhouse.

"It's the guys," Roderick said, pointing. "They're right up ahead on that roof with a tree sticking out of it."

She looked where he was pointing and began to wave, too.

"They sure look happy to see us," she said. "I woulda thought for sure they'd be mad."

Roderick danced around, waving his arms above his head and doing the same kind of crazy, pointing dance he saw Tom and Percival doing on the rooftop ahead. He took a big bite from his potato as he swiveled his hips.

"Hey, what are you eating?" Abbey asked, her voice going cold. Roderick tried to hide the half-eaten vegetable behind his back, but he lost his grip.

"Is that a potato?" Abbey asked. "What did we tell you about eating the potatoes!"

Ignoring the little Bone's rant, Roderick spun around and leaned out over the bow, trying to snag his treat before it was gone. But he wasn't fast enough, and instead watched as the potato bounced off the head of one of two Rat Creatures dangling from the anchor, before continuing to tumble to the ground far below.

Rat Creatures!

Roderick let out a scream and sprang away from the side of the *Queen*.

"You better scream," Abbey said. "That was a perfectly good potato you just wasted."

Roderick was so scared he couldn't speak. His mouth was moving, but no words came out as he frantically pointed over the side of the ship.

"What are you trying to say?" she asked. "I saw you drop it, but there's no use crying over it now; you've got to make sure that —" Abbey started, and then stopped as she stuck her head over the side and saw them — big, fat, nasty, and hairy, clinging to their sky ship's anchor.

And she began to scream, and scream, and scream. . . .

"There she goes," Percival said, scrunching up his face and sticking his fingers in his ears.

Tom winced, too. There was panic on board the *Queen of the Sky*, but he had other problems to deal with at the moment.

Standing at the roof's edge, he looked over the side to the ground below. The Constable and his monstrous deputies had gathered outside the jail, and it appeared that they had a different plan now. They were dragging bushels of hay from the marketplace and laying them against the building's foundation.

"This isn't good," Tom said. He looked back up at the *Queen of the Sky* still gradually drawing closer. He could make out the shapes of Abbey and Roderick running around in a panic over the discovery of their hairy stowaways.

Tom smelled a trace of something burning, and he looked down to see the first of the hay piles being ignited.

Orange tongues of fire were lapping at the jail and quickly blazing higher and higher.

"These guys mean business," Percival said.

"Whatever possesses them is made from the darkest of evils," the Veni Yan priest commented. "The depth of their depravity knows no bounds."

As thick black smoke billowed up into the air, they were distracted by the sounds of more screaming. This time it wasn't Abbey but the Rat Creatures, swinging from the anchor below the *Queen*.

Screaming because they were under attack.

"We've got to knock them off!" Roderick cried.

Abbey was in a panic, running as far from the bow of the ship as possible. "What are those things?" she asked, her voice shaking with fear.

"Those are Rat Creatures," Roderick said. "They're horrible monsters that'll eat us up if they get on this ship."

"We've got to get rid of them!" she said, jumping up and down anxiously.

"Right," Roderick said. "We've just got to figure out how." He looked around the ship.

"Hurry up!" Abbey said. "I don't want those things to eat me."

"I've got it," Roderick said.

Barclay emerged from the wheelhouse. "What's goin' on out here?" he asked. "You think it's easy flying a sky ship with all that racket?"

"We got Rat Creatures," Abbey said.

"We got what?" the boy Bone asked in confusion. He looked at Roderick, who pointed over the side of the *Queen*.

"Take a look," the raccoon said.

"I leave you two alone for a few minutes and . . ." Barclay began as he joined Roderick.

The two hairy beasts were looking up at them, and one actually waved.

"AAAARRRGH!" Barclay screamed, falling back.

"Told ya," Roderick said.

"We got Rat Creatures and we have to get rid of them." Abbey was still frantic.

"What should we do?" Barclay asked, equally panicked.

"We throw stuff at 'em until they fall off," the raccoon explained.

"What kind of stuff?" Abbey asked.

Roderick dropped to all fours and ran behind the wheelhouse. He reappeared quickly, dragging a wooden crate of potatoes behind him.

"We can't throw those," Abbey protested. "How will we power the ship?"

"There's more crates below deck, but we can't worry about that right now," Roderick said, hefting a potato in each hand.

Barclay armed himself next, and then Abbey.

"Uncle Percival isn't going to be too happy about this," she warned.

"Then make sure you don't waste a shot," the raccoon said, spinning around and darting to the side.

"Take that!" he cried, letting the first of his potatoes fly at the ratty targets. "That's for my mother," he growled as it struck one of the Rats in the face.

"And this is for my dad!" The second potato bounced off the other Hairy Man's head.

The Rat Creatures held tight, but there were many more potatoes left to throw.

CHAPTER 13

There was chaos aboard the *Queen of the Sky*.

The sky craft's progress had slowed, and Percival guessed that the ship's automatic pilot had been engaged.

He and Tom could see Roderick, Abbey, and Barclay running around the deck, each of them taking turns throwing things over the side of the ship, trying to knock the Rat Creatures from their perch.

"What in the name of refried beans are they pitchin'?" Percival asked.

"It looks like big rocks," Tom said, squinting.

"Big rocks?" Percival asked. "Where would they find big rocks on board the *Queen* unless . . ." The Bone adventurer paused for a moment before it hit him. "They're throwing my potatoes!" he cried.

Percival ran as close as he could to the edge of the roof, waving away the black smoke that rose up from the burning building. "Hey, you kids, stop throwing them spuds this instant!" he hollered. "Do ya hear me?"

The building began to creak and moan as the fire ate hungrily at its lower foundation and supports. Then a huge wave of fire roared up from the side of the building, nearly knocking Percival from the edge. Tom managed to grab hold of his collar and yank him back.

"Thanks," the Bone said, tapping down the smoldering lapels of his shirt pockets. "That was a little too close for comfort."

"It's all going to be a little too close for comfort if we don't get off this roof," Tom said.

The *Queen* had drifted closer, but still not close enough.

And the flames had grown dangerously high, burning on all four sides of the jail, surrounding them with fire. The building shuddered, and Tom knew it wouldn't be long before the entire roof caved in. Instinctively, he reached up and grabbed hold of what he'd once believed to be his lucky rock.

"I know you picked me to be your champion and everything, and I'm trying not to disappoint you, but we could really use your help here," Tom said, waiting for a response as the flames grew hotter, and higher.

Barclay returned to the deck with another crate.

"Here are more," he said, pulling back the wooden

cover with a loud creak. Roderick and Abbey rushed forward, each grabbing a handful.

"I think I saw one of them start to slip," the raccoon said as he returned to the side of the ship.

"Which one?" Abbey asked. "I'll aim at that one, too."

Barclay grabbed a couple of potatoes and joined them.

"We should all throw at the same time and —"

"Barclay," a strange and tiny voice cried out.

The boy stopped and looked around. "Hello?"

"Barclay," said the voice again.

"Where are you?" he asked. He recognized the woman's voice but couldn't pinpoint the source. "I can't see you."

"In your hand," directed the voice.

Barclay looked at the potato he was holding and gasped.

A face had formed in the surface of the lumpy vegetable, a face that he recognized as belonging to the strange plant woman called Lorimar.

"Hey, how'd you get your face on my potato?" Barclay asked in amazement.

"All things of root, vine, and earth are mine to control," Lorimar said. "But there is little time for explanation."

Barclay held the potato up for his sister and friend to see.

"Hey, guys, look at this!" he called. Abbey and Roderick left their targets and stepped closer.

"Is that Lorimar?" the raccoon asked, reaching out with his paw.

"Don't touch her," Barclay said, pulling it away. "I think she has something important to tell us."

They all looked at the face on the potato, waiting to hear what she had to say.

"Do not concern yourselves with the Rat Creatures," she said. "Quickly, retrieve Tom Elm and the others, for their safety is at risk."

Barclay handed the potato to his sister. "Here, hold this," he said.

He walked to the bow of the ship and looked out over the village. For the first time, he noticed the thick, black smoke and the fire burning the building below it.

And his friends trapped on the roof.

"Oh my gosh," he cried, running to the wheelhouse and switching off the autopilot function. His small hands flew over the control panel as he desperately tried to remember what he'd so recently taught himself.

He hoped he wasn't too late.

The Constable smiled as he watched the flames grow higher and higher. The Nacht had been quite specific about making sure that the boy and the former warrior did not continue their quest, and they had already failed to stop Tom Elm once. The Spark could not be reassembled, for it would surely mean the end of his spirit brothers and their glorious master, the Nacht. Gazing up at the burning structure, he felt supremely confident that he and his brethren had finally succeeded.

They would not fail their master again.

The fire had grown so intense and the smoke so thick that he could no longer see his foes trapped upon the roof. He imagined them up there, frightened and cursing themselves for ever thinking they could stand against the power of the Nacht.

The building moaned, gradually surrendering to the voracious flames. It wouldn't be long until the jail collapsed.

The Constable's spirit brothers joined him, all of them sharing in their victory over the young hero. That's when the Constable heard it, the strangest of sounds — a humming, like the voices of a thousand bees. It was coming from behind him, and he turned from the fire to see a shocking sight in the sky above them.

"What is it?" one of his brothers asked, as they all looked up at the large ship overhead.

"And what are they?" another one asked, pointing at the two hairy beasts hanging from beneath the great wooden vessel.

The Constable suddenly realized that it was all about to go very wrong.

"You need to do what I tell you," Lorimar said from the potato in Abbey's hand.

"I've never talked to a potato before," the little girl said. "I once sang to an ice-cream sundae, but that was only because I was happy."

"You must bring me to the *Queen*'s side."

"Over here?" Abbey asked, running across the deck, Roderick and Barclay at her heels.

"Where the Rat Creatures are?" the raccoon asked.

"Yes, exactly," Lorimar said. "And you must take careful aim and throw me at them, as hard as you can."

"I bet I can throw harder than her," Barclay said.

"Can not," Abbey retorted.

"Children, please," Lorimar begged. "Time is of the essence." She knew there was no room for failure. It was only a matter of seconds before the building succumbed to the flames, and Tom and the others would be lost.

The servants of the Nacht had to be distracted, and Lorimar required the unwitting assistance of the two Rat Creatures to make her plan work.

"Throw me, child!" Lorimar screamed, as loud as a potato was able. "Throw me now!"

Abbey did exactly as she was told, and Lorimar opened what passed for a mouth on the lumpy surface of the vegetable, ready to bite.

The potato struck one of the Rats on the upper arm, and she bit down through the thick, matted fur, pinching the tender flesh there.

The Rat Creature shrieked, flailing his arms and losing his grip on the anchor. The Other Rat Creature attempted to help his partner, and quickly found himself in a similar predicament.

They both began to fall.

Tom couldn't see a thing. The smoke from the burning building had become so thick and choking that he'd lost sight of the *Queen*.

"What are we gonna do now?" Percival asked between coughs.

Tom felt a tremor through the soles of his boots, telling him that the building was about to fall.

"We accept our fate and know that we fought bravely," the Veni Yan priest said, but Tom wasn't ready to admit defeat. He refused to believe that the Dreaming would abandon them now, after they'd already been through so much.

And still had so much to do.

The roof beneath them shuddered for what would likely be a final time, as Tom tried to squint through the roiling smoke before him. *If only I could see . . .*

And see he did. Something was moving very quickly

through the noxious cloud, something darker than the smoke itself. In a split second, he realized what was coming toward them, and knew that there was a chance they were about to be saved.

"Get ready!" Tom yelled as the anchor emerged from the smoke, the monstrous Hairy Men no longer hanging from it.

Tom grabbed hold as the heavy anchor passed, and hoped that his friends had managed to do the same. Just then, there was a deafening roar, and the roof dropped out from beneath them in a shower of orange sparks, dust, and debris.

Holding on for dear life, Tom twisted in the smoky air.

"Percival!" he cried out. "Percival, are you there?"

For a moment, there was silence, and Tom feared the worst, but then he heard the Bone adventurer's distinct voice.

"I'm here," he said, though sounding a little odd. "We both are . . . me and the priest . . . but I'm not sure for how much longer."

Once they were pulled from the blinding smoke, Tom could see Percival gripping the lower half of the anchor with both hands, and the Veni Yan desperately hanging on to him.

By one of his ankles.

The countryside flew by far beneath them as they soared above it. If they were to fall . . .

Tom didn't want to think about it; he had to do something to help his friends.

Swallowing the possibility that he might plummet to his death, Tom adjusted his grip on the anchor and reached a trembling hand out to the Bone.

"Can you take my hand?" Tom asked.

"Afraid I'll fall if I let go," Percival grunted. "Which doesn't mean . . . I'm not gonna . . . fall . . . anyway," the Bone adventurer gasped with exertion.

"Hold on," Tom urged, as he shinnied farther down the length of the anchor and again reached out. "Here," he said. But Percival didn't move, and Tom watched with horror as the explorer's fingers began to slip. Tom let himself slide even farther down and grabbed hold of one of Percival's hands just as the Bone lost his grip.

"Got ya!" Tom exclaimed excitedly, his exuberance short-lived as the excessive weight proved far too much for him, and he was yanked from the anchor.

As they fell, Tom tensed his body, bracing himself for the amazing pain that would come when he hit the ground. But it wouldn't feel half as bad as the pain he was already feeling for letting his friends — and the Dreaming — down. Roderick had been right all this time; he was nothing but a turnip farmer, and would always be one.

If he survived, that is.

But the drop wasn't nearly as catastrophic as he'd imagined it would be. To his surprise, he and his friends landed within the comforting embrace of a large oak tree, its bountiful leaves cushioning them from the worst of the fall.

"Is everybody all right?" Tom asked, using the tree's thick branches to climb down.

"Good thing this tree was here or we would have been splattered across the countryside," Percival said as Tom helped the Bone to the ground. "Funny, I don't remember seeing a tree this big from up in the air," he added, laying a hand upon its trunk.

"Yeah, neither do I," Tom agreed, an idea of its origin beginning to form in his mind.

"No matter," the warrior priest said, dropping down to the ground with a grunt, in a shower of leaves and acorns. "It was here, and that's all that matters."

The trunk of the tree started to crack and split as a familiar face began to form there.

"Hello, Lorimar," Tom said, happy to see that she was all right and that his suspicions were correct. "Thanks for the oak tree," he said.

"I am glad to help," she said.

"I shoulda known you had something to do with it," Percival said, shielding his eyes to look up at the tree. "She's a beauty."

The *Queen of the Sky* temporarily blotted out the sun as it flew in a circle above their heads.

"And speaking of beauties," the Bone adventurer said, and started to signal to the craft.

Tom could feel the warrior priest's curious eyes on him. "Who are you people?" the Veni Yan asked with wonder.

"I'm Tom Elm, this is Percival Bone, and this is Lorimar," Tom said, pointing to the tree. "We were sent to rescue you."

"By the Dreaming?" he asked, bewildered by the idea.

"Yes," Tom answered him. "We've been chosen for a very important mission . . . and so have you."

CHAPTER 14

Once Tom, Percival, and the warrior priest had climbed the rope ladder up onto the *Queen of the Sky*, the twins ran straight to their uncle and hugged him with all their might.

"You're not mad at us for flying the *Queen*, are you, Unc?" Barclay asked, gazing up at his uncle, his arms wrapped around Percival's waist.

"No, I'm not mad," Percival said, hugging them in return. "Matter of fact, I'm mighty impressed."

"If I was you, I'd want to tan our bottoms good," Abbey said.

"Then it's a good thing I'm not you, isn't it?"

They all hugged again, and Tom smiled for a moment before looking out over the side. Lorimar's face had vanished from the trunk of the tree, and he wondered if she was back in the body of the *Queen*.

The Veni Yan plucked some leaves from the sleeves of his robes, and Tom noticed an acorn fall to the deck. When it came to a stop, it began to bounce up and down.

Everyone fell quiet and watched, fascinated. In seconds the oak nut had cracked, tendrils of leafy green snaking from the broken shell across the deck, growing by leaps and bounds. It was as if time had sped up and Tom was watching a tree grow to maturity right before his eyes. But what started out to be a tree took a dramatic turn when it began to take the form of a woman.

Lorimar, wearing the guise of the mighty oak, stood silent upon the deck before slowly raising her leafy head to look at them all.

"Much better," she said, holding out her branchlike arms to admire her latest form. Tom had to agree — he liked this shape much better than a face in the side of the ship.

Tom was feeling uneasy.

They had managed to save the Veni Yan priest and to return in one piece, but something still wasn't quite right. It gnawed at him, almost as if he was forgetting something.

Or somebody.

"Is there a problem, Tom?" Lorimar asked.

"No . . ." he said, looking out over the countryside. "I

don't know," he continued, confused. "I get the feeling that something isn't right. That this mission isn't complete."

He looked at the oak woman, hoping for an answer.

"Perhaps you should listen to these feelings," she said.

Tom was about to question her further when Roderick came to his side and gave him a poke.

"What's his name?" Roderick asked in a whisper, pointing at the Veni Yan priest who sat away from them, by himself. They had given him some water when they'd first arrived on ship, and then he'd gone off on his own.

Tom shrugged his shoulders. "I don't know, but if he's going to join us, I should probably find out."

He and Roderick approached the man together. Tom was about to speak when Roderick began.

"Hi," the raccoon said. "My name's Roderick; what's yours?"

The man seemed to be in deep thought, but his serious features blossomed into a smile for the small animal. "Hello, Roderick." He reached out, taking Roderick's tiny paw in his hand. "My name is Randolf . . . Randolf Clearmeadow."

"Randolf Clearmeadow," the raccoon repeated, letting the two names roll over his tongue. "That's a very nice name."

The warrior priest smiled again. "What an odd bunch,"

he said with a chuckle, taking a sip of water from his metal cup. "And you tell me that we're all supposed to be going on some sort of quest?" He laughed again with a shake of his head.

Tom was about to explain when he felt it again, a feeling of unfinished business, this time stronger than before. The shard of Spark that hung around his neck flashed momentarily, and he reached up to touch it. A sudden flash of images made him gasp aloud.

He saw them all together — Roderick, Lorimar, the Bones, the Veni Yan priest — but in this vision two more had been added to the group.

"I've got it! I know what's wrong," he said.

"Everything okay, Tom?" Percival asked.

Tom nodded, his mind suddenly clear. "I'm fine," he said. "I understand what the Dreaming has been trying to tell me."

This seemed to pique Randolf's curiosity.

"The Dreaming actually talks to you?" he asked.

"It's guiding me with visions," Tom explained. "Trying to help me get everything in place so we can stop the Nacht from carrying out its plans."

"And what, pray tell, are this Nacht's plans?" the Veni Yan asked.

"Everything covered in darkness," the boy said,

shuddering. "It wants the Valley, and then the world, to become one never-ending nightmare."

"The Dreaming has told you this?" Randolf asked.

"It has," Tom said. "And it sent me to rescue you, and now it's telling me that there are two more that need to join us."

"Two more, Tom?" Roderick asked. "Who?"

"We've already encountered them, I'm afraid to say."

His friends all looked confused.

"Who are we talking about here, Tom?" Percival wanted to know.

"The Rat Creatures," Tom said. "Remember how I saw them in my earlier vision? Well, I saw them again. They're supposed to be with us."

Everyone, except Lorimar, looked at him as if he'd lost his mind.

"What are you, crazy?" Roderick cried. "We can't have those monsters on board. They can't be trusted."

"I have to agree with Roderick, Tom," Percival said. "From what I hear, those things are pretty nasty, and unpredictable."

"There's no way I want those monsters on board my ship," Abbey said, her brother nodding fiercely beside her.

"Is there any chance you might be mistaken, boy?" Randolf asked.

Tom thought for a moment, but he knew that this was how it was supposed to be. They all had a part to play in this quest, even the Rats.

"I'm not mistaken," Tom said with a slight shake of his head. "The Rat Creatures have to join us."

The old man's face was a dark mask as he considered this, and then abruptly he turned and walked away.

"I can't believe you want to do this," Roderick said. "You know what they're like . . . what they did to my mom and dad."

"I know, Roderick, and I'm sorry, but the Dreaming —"

"The Dreaming is wrong," Roderick yelled, his voice trembling. The raccoon turned and ran off to the wheel-house, the sound of his tiny feet on the stairs to the hold drifting out to them.

"Percival, I . . ." Tom began.

"I don't know about this one, Tom," the Bone said, rubbing his chin. "It was crazy enough that you got me to participate in this rescue attempt of yours, but now you want to bring those things on board and risk the safety of everyone here. I just don't know."

"I think the Dreaming is making a mistake," Abbey chimed in.

"I do, too," Barclay said, and for once Tom saw the pair in agreement.

Is it possible? he wondered. *Could the Dreaming be wrong? Or do I just not understand what it's trying to tell me?*

"Lorimar," Tom said, turning to the forest woman, who had been quiet the whole time. "I don't know what to do," he said.

"You must do what you feel . . . what you know is right," she said, making him feel all the more troubled.

"I know they're monsters," Tom told the others. "But they do have a part to play in this mission . . . an important part if the Dreaming needs them to be here with us." Tom made eye contact with each of them as he tried to show how strongly he felt about this. "I trust the Dreaming," he added.

"And so do I," Randolf said, as he turned from where he'd been standing near the side of the *Queen*. "It has been quite some time since the Dreaming and I last spoke, but something tells me . . . a feeling at my very core . . . that this boy speaks the truth."

"So you think we should go back and get the Rat Creatures?" Percival asked.

"I do not," Randolf said. "But this boy, the chosen of the Dreaming, does. And although I find the beasts incredibly vile, and the bane of all life in the Valley, if they have a part to play in this quest, I believe we must allow them to do it."

"Thank you, Randolf," Tom said.

"Don't thank me, boy. For it is the captain of this vessel who will have the last word on whether or not the Rats will be allowed on board."

Percival Bone was pacing and stroking his chin, deep in thought.

"Don't do it, Unc," Barclay warned. "Those things gobbled up poor Roderick's parents."

"And who knows, they might've eaten our parents, too!" Abbey cried.

Percival looked away from his niece's and nephew's pleading eyes and met Tom's. "Are you sure about this?"

"As sure as I am about anything these days," Tom replied. He couldn't think of anything more to say to convince them.

The Bone adventurer nodded. "All right, then," he said, walking toward the wheelhouse. "Let me turn her around."

Barclay's and Abbey's faces scrunched up with anger and disappointment, and both stomped off to join Roderick in the ship's hold.

"I hope I'm right about this," Tom muttered beneath his breath.

"I hope you are, too," Randolf responded, patting the boy on the shoulder before going off to again be alone.

Tom looked to Lorimar, hoping for some words of encouragement, but the forest woman remained eerily silent, like a tree standing in the woods.

The Rats were frantic.

First they'd offended their King by stealing the dead squirrel, which resulted in their being chased by the King's guard, and just when they thought they'd made the right decision to capture the great sky wagon with all its delicious occupants, they were hauled up into the sky and dangled above the countryside, pelted by potatoes, and dropped down into the midst of human villagers who really didn't seem quite so human anymore.

Frantic? Oh yes.

And now these humans who weren't so human were trying to kill them, while their prize had sailed off with two humans and a Bone.

The Rats tried to explain that they were having a really bad day, but the inhuman humans didn't want to hear it.

So the Rat Creatures ran, darting between the village structures, with those who were eager to slay them in pursuit.

They had to get to the forest. The sun would be setting soon, and in the darkness of night, they could escape their pursuers — perhaps even capturing one or two as a gift for their King. It wasn't a sky wagon, but it would have to do.

"I think we should capture a few of these strange humans and offer them to King Agak," the Rat Creature said while hiding behind a stable, trying to catch his breath.

"Wasn't it you that had the bright idea of taking the sky wagon?" the Other asked. "And we saw how well that worked out."

"No, I think this might be what we need to get back in his good graces. I bet these humans taste completely different from the normal kind."

"I think we should just throw ourselves at his mercy, and offer him back the squirrel," the Other said. "Perhaps our punishment won't be so bad."

The Rat Creature recoiled, holding his beloved dead varmint to his chest. "Give him Fredrick? I wouldn't dream of it after all we've been through. There are dead squirrels and there are dead squirrels," the Rat Creature scolded his friend. "And Fredrick is a very special dead squirrel."

"Quiet," the Other hissed. "The inhumans are coming."

"Quickly," the Rat said. "We probably have enough time to reach the woods."

They were halfway across the broad expanse of ground that separated them from freedom when the heated cries began.

"There they are!" one of the odd humans cried.

"Get them before they escape!" bellowed another.

"Make them pay for interfering with the Nacht's plans!" said a third.

The odd humans rushed at them, swords and knives raised above their heads in fury.

"Don't be afraid, Fredrick," the Rat Creature said to his squirrel. "I won't let anything happen to you."

"Oh, sure, you won't let anything happen to the squirrel, but what about me?"

"You can take care of yourself; Fredrick's just a little bit of a thing."

The darkness of the woods beckoned to them. They bounded into the concealing forest, then came to a sudden stop, their nocturnal eyes scanning the darkness for signs of movement.

"Did you see that?" the Rat Creature asked his comrade.

"I think so," the Other hissed.

"You come out this instant," the Rat Creature demanded, reaching out to part a growth of thick bushes before them. "Can't you see we're running for our lives?"

King Agak and ten of his ferocious soldiers glared back at him.

"YEEEEK!" the Rat Creature screeched.

"AAAAGGGH!" screamed the Other.

The pair immediately spun around, leaping from the

cover of the dark forest — and came face-to-face with the humans who weren't quite human, their razor-sharp weapons glistening sharply in the light of the rising moon.

"YEEEEK!" the Rat Creature screeched again.

"AAAAGGGH!" reiterated the Other.

The leader of the inhumans smiled. "Stop right there, monsters," he growled, looking down the length of his blade. "There is much you must pay for."

Slowly the Rats started to back up, turning to see the King and his followers stalking toward them.

"Wake me up, will you?" Agak bellowed. "Steal my squirrel carcass . . . the gall of it all. You two shall soon learn the error of your ways."

The Rats stopped again, not sure where to go, with humans who weren't really human on one side of them and their furious King and his bloodthirsty soldiers on the other.

Oh yes, they were in for some big trouble.

"I want you to have this," the Rat Creature said, shoving Fredrick into the Other's hand.

"You want me to have . . . to have Fredrick?"

"I do," the Rat Creature said. "Maybe if they think you were responsible for the whole thing, the King will go easy on me."

"Have I ever mentioned how much I loathe you?" the

Other asked, raising the dead squirrel above his head. He was ready to pummel his betrayer with the corpse when an unfamiliar voice called out.

"Hey, you two!"

The Rats looked around, confused, as their enemies grew ever closer.

"Up here," called the mysterious voice again.

They looked up and gasped, so startled that they grabbed hold of each other in a fear-filled embrace.

The sky wagon was floating in the air above their heads, the human boy they had seen rescued from the burning building calling down to them.

"Looks like you two are in quite the predicament," the boy said.

The Rat Creatures watched their troubles come increasingly closer and had to agree.

"I have an offer for you," the boy said.

The Rats gazed up at him, waiting to hear his proposal.

"I'll get you out of here, but you have to promise to behave," he said.

The Rats looked at each other, and then back up to the boy.

"What do you mean by behave, exactly?" the Rat Creature asked.

"You have to be on your best behavior," the boy explained. "And not hurt or eat anybody on board this ship."

The Rats looked at each other again.

"It is asking quite a bit," the Other said with a shake of his head. "I don't know."

The inhumans were almost upon them. "Prepare to be skinned alive!" the leader bellowed, waving his blade.

"Prepare to suffer for the insults you have perpetrated against me!" cried King Agak, as he and his soldiers closed in.

The Rats looked up at the boy hanging out of the sky wagon.

"We'll behave," they said as one.

"Do you promise?" the boy asked, grabbing a rope ladder.

"We promise," they agreed.

"And if we break that promise, you can have this dead squirrel," the Other said, holding the corpse up for the boy to see.

"How dare you offer to give Fredrick away," the Rat Creature said, stunned.

"Shut up and grab the rope," the Other commanded as the ladder dropped down in front of them.

"I want him back," the Rat Creature informed his comrade as he took hold of the ladder's rungs. "Giving him to you was a terrible mistake."

"We'll just have to see," the Other said, also taking hold

of the ladder. "I think Freddy is starting to like me more."

"Fredrick, how could you?" the Rat Creature asked, stifling his tears as the sky wagon drifted higher, lifting the pair from harm's way.

King Agak hissed ferociously, the hair on his back prickling in anger at the group of humans who now challenged them. His Rat soldiers grumbled and growled, awaiting his command to attack, but it did not come.

There was something strange about these humans, the Rat Creature King thought as he sniffed the air. There was no stink of fear from them, which was curious, for there was always fear when their kind came face-to-face.

The King lunged with a growl, but the humans didn't move. They stood their ground, staring oddly with their weapons in hand. Yes, there was definitely something different about these humans, something that told Agak it would be wise to beware.

"Why you chase rogue rats?" the King asked, having difficulty speaking the human language.

"They allowed our enemies to escape," the leader said, speaking the language of the Rat Creatures perfectly. "They should be punished."

King Agak was impressed; these humans were truly strange indeed.

"The ones that flew away with the traitors," he said, pointing with a claw up into the night sky. "Are they your enemies?"

The leader nodded, his eyes as dark as a cave opening.

"We seek the rogues to punish them, so those that fly are our enemies as well," Agak said.

The leader smiled as he realized what the King was getting at.

"You wish to join our forces?" the leader asked.

Normally, the King despised humans and everything they stood for, but there was something about these particular men, something that made him want to work with them.

"Yes," King Agak agreed. "Join forces."

"Excellent," the leader said between bouts of laughter.

Something dark whispered in the King's ear that this was right.

The *Queen of the Sky* sailed through the night, its controls on automatic as the captain helped deal with the newest passengers.

The two Rat Creatures had been herded into a corner of the deck, behind the wheelhouse. They cowered as the others glared at them. Percival wasn't exactly sure who was more afraid of who.

"Don't get too close now," Percival warned, his hands gripping Abbey's and Barclay's shoulders.

"They're ugly," Abbey said, wrinkling her nose. "And they don't smell so good, either."

"They don't look so tough," Barclay said, shaking his tiny fist at the beasts. "And if they know better, they won't give us a hard time."

Percival gave his nephew's shoulder a squeeze.

"Don't be starting any trouble now," he told the boy. "They're behaving, just like Tom asked them."

"Hmmph." Abbey crossed her arms over her chest. "I still don't understand why Tom had to bring them on board. Look at 'em. What can they do to help us?"

Randolf was suddenly standing beside them, his intense gaze fixed on the two Rat Creatures.

"Never underestimate the Rats, child," he said. "That was my failing so very long ago. I thought of them as stupid beasts, never imagining that they would have the intelligence and cunning to challenge us, and to take away all that I lived for."

The Rats began to growl, sensing the powerful emotions that were radiating from the man. Randolf slowly withdrew a nasty-looking dagger from within his faded robes.

"Easy there, pal," Percival warned.

"Have no worry, friend," he said, eyes still locked upon the beastly pair. "No harm will come to these two unless they give us no choice. Remember, they have been chosen by the Dreaming."

The Rat Creatures looked at each other.

"Did you hear that, comrade?" the Rat Creature whispered to his companion.

"I did," the Other Rat answered. "Something about being chosen by the Dreaming."

"I know of no such choosing," the Rat Creature said. "What could they be talking about?"

The Other shrugged his shoulders, just as Barclay darted forward.

"Barclay!" Percival cried, reaching for his nephew, but the boy was too fast.

"You were chosen, all right," the little Bone said, staring the Rats up and down. "It's the only reason why you're on my uncle's sky ship. Tom said that he had a vision about you two, and that you're supposed to help us."

The Rats glanced at each other again, and then back at the boy.

"Help?" said one.

"How?" said the Other.

"I don't know yet," Barclay told them. "But you're gonna help us with our quest when we need you."

Percival pulled the boy back to stand with his sister.

"What, are you a dope or something?" she asked. "They could have eaten you just like they did Roderick's parents."

"They ain't so tough," Barclay said. "They know who's boss."

One of the Rat's raised his hand. "Ah, who is the boss?" he asked nervously. "Is it the boy that offered us rescue?"

"Yeah, that's Tom," Percival told them. "The leader of our motley crew."

"Tom," both Rats repeated, as if memorizing the name.

"Yeah, he's the leader of the quest," Abbey said. "Hey, if you two are gonna be part of our group, what should we call you?"

"Call us?" the Rat Creature asked.

"Yeah, what are your names?" the little girl asked. "I'm Abbey, and this is my little brother, Barclay," she said, pointing to her brother.

"I'm not your little brother, we're twins," he corrected her.

"But I was born first," she quickly responded.

"Not this again," the boy said, slapping a palm against his head.

"Names?" the Rat Creature asked, placing a claw to the corner of his mouth.

"Well, this is Fredrick," the Other said, holding out the rotting remains of the dead squirrel.

"I call him traitor," said the Other's companion angrily.

"No, what are your names?" Abbey asked, looking annoyed. She placed her hands on her hips.

"The lesser Rats have no names," Randolf said. "Only the royalty of their kind are given names."

"He's right," the Other said.

"Well, that'll be way too confusing," Barclay said. "We're just gonna have to give you names."

"They're going to give us names," the Rat Creature said as he jammed his elbow into the Other's side. "Isn't it exciting?"

"I want to name them!" Abbey roared, stomping her foot down hard upon the deck.

"All right, all right, don't get yourself in a lather," Percival said. "You can each name one. Go ahead, Barclay, you first."

Abbey scowled as the little boy's forehead wrinkled in thought. "I think I'm gonna call you . . ." He paused, pointing at the most excited of the pair.

"Yes?"

"I'm gonna call you Stinky," he said.

"Stinky?" the Rat Creature repeated. "I'm not feeling it."

The Other Rat burst out laughing, waving the dead animal. "Stinky . . . that's perfect."

It was Abbey's turn.

"And I'm gonna call you . . ." she said, addressing the Other Rat.

The Other stopped laughing, looking at the girl expectantly.

"Smelly," she said with a happy nod.

The two Rats regarded each other.

"Smelly?" said Stinky.

"Stinky?" said Smelly.

"Perfect," said the Bone brother and sister, excited that they had agreed to something without fighting.

"Well, that's it, then," Percival said cheerfully. "Welcome aboard, Stinky and Smelly."

"Yes, welcome aboard," Randolf Clearmeadow said menacingly, still holding on to the grip of his dagger. "And watch your behavior well."

Tom sat on one of the last crates of potatoes in the *Queen*'s hold, waiting for his best friend to forgive him.

He'd been waiting for a while.

"So you're not even going to talk to me?" he asked, facing a dark corner where there was a large spool of rope. Roderick was behind it.

Tom could hear the sound of voices from the deck above and wondered what they were talking about. It didn't sound as if anything violent was going on, so the two Rat

Creatures must have been living up to their promise.

"C'mon, Roderick," he tried again. "You know I wouldn't do anything on purpose to make you sad."

"Well, you're still doing a very good job," the raccoon said from his hiding place. His voice sounded very small.

"I know Rat Creatures killed your parents, but in order to be ready for this quest, I have to do everything the Dreaming shows me."

"Even if it's dangerous?" Roderick asked. "Even if it could mean our lives?"

Tom sighed. He knew exactly where his friend was going with this. The Rats were trouble, there was no doubt about it, but the Dreaming wanted them. That meant they had a purpose in finding the pieces of the first Spark.

"They promised to behave if we saved them," the boy explained.

"Oh, and Rat Creatures never lie," the raccoon said sarcastically.

"I didn't say that," Tom retorted, frustrated that he couldn't get through to his friend.

"Then how can you trust them, Tom?" Roderick asked, emerging from behind the coiled rope. The little guy's eyes were red, the fur beneath them damp. "How do you know that they're not gonna hurt you, or Abbey, or Barclay?"

Tom had to be honest. "I don't," he said, throwing up

his hands. "But I saw them in my vision as clear as day. . . . I even saw that one of them was carrying a dead squirrel. I have to trust that the Dreaming knows what it's talking about."

The little raccoon's shoulders slumped as fat tears rolled from his eyes. "But what if the Dreaming's wrong?"

"It can't be," Tom said, getting up and going to his friend. He plopped down on the floor and put his arm around the raccoon. "'Cause if it is, it's wrong about the rest of us being able to stop the Nacht from spreading across the Valley and out into the whole wide world, and we can't believe a thing like that, can we?"

Roderick finally hugged him back, wiping his runny raccoon nose on the shoulder of Tom's tunic.

"No, we can't," his animal friend said. "We've got to stop the Nacht so that our family wakes up."

"Our family and all those poor people in Trumble, and all the other places the Nacht might've already touched."

"We can't let it happen to anyone else," Roderick said with a shake of his head.

"No, we can't," Tom agreed. "So, are we still best friends?"

Roderick thought about it for a moment.

"Only if the Rat Creatures don't eat us in our sleep," he said.

"Then we'll just have to make sure that never happens," Tom told him, climbing to his feet. He held a hand out to his friend. "Shall we go up on deck and plan what we're doing next?" he asked.

"Yeah," Roderick answered, placing his tiny paw in Tom's hand. "We've got a bigger job to do than picking turnips."

"We certainly do," Tom said, and together they left to rejoin the others.

Tom felt it as soon as he was back on deck; the shard of the Spark that he wore around his neck was glowing.

"What is it?" Roderick asked as the boy released the raccoon's paw.

"It's glowing again," Tom said, reaching inside his tunic to pull out the stone, which still hung from the leather thong. The others were watching him, curious.

"The last time it did this, I touched it, and it gave me a vision," the boy explained.

"Well, go ahead and touch it," Percival told him. "Might give us a better idea as to what we're up to next."

Tom looked to Lorimar, who had continued to stand quietly, away from the others. "Is that what it wants me to do?" he asked her.

"Go ahead." She gestured with a wave of her branch-like limbs. "Only the Dreaming can tell you."

"All right, here goes," he said with a sigh. He held his breath, counted to three, and wrapped his right hand around the pulsing white stone and . . .

Felt nothing.

"Well?" Percival asked.

"Did the Dreaming communicate with you again?" Randolf asked.

"Can we go now?" asked one of the Rat Creatures, the other one quickly shushing him.

"I got nothing," Tom said, opening his hand to look at the stone. It was still glowing, pulsing with an eerie inner light, as if it had a heartbeat. "It doesn't glow like this all the time. I wonder what it's trying to tell me."

"YEEEEEKKKKKKKKK!"

One of the Rats suddenly began to scream, and everybody's attention turned to the furry beast. It was the Rat Creature that had been carrying the dead squirrel. He tossed the rotting animal to the deck and cowered behind his friend.

"What's wrong with you?" Tom asked.

"Yeah, Smelly," Barclay echoed. "What's wrong with you?"

"Smelly?" Tom questioned.

"Yeah, that one's Smelly, and the other one's Stinky," Barclay explained.

Tom shook his head, knowing immediately who had

named them, but not why Smelly was so frightened.

"What is it, Smelly?" the Rat Creature asked his companion.

"It's Fredrick," Smelly said with a tremble of fear in his voice. "He . . . he's glowing."

Stinky dropped to the deck and slunk closer to the squirrel carcass. He was giving the body a good sniff when it happened — a sudden pulse of light from beneath the dead animal's skin. He gasped, recoiling.

"You're right," he told his companion. "Fredrick is glowing. . . . I hope he's not sick," the Rat Creature fretted.

Tom watched the squirrel for another sign, and didn't have long to wait. A weak light shone through what remained of the dead animal's fur and skin, a light that pulsed in time with the shard around Tom's own neck.

He stepped closer.

"Careful, Tom," Percival warned. "We don't know what's happening there."

"I think I do," the boy responded. "We need to open it up."

"I think I'm going to faint," Stinky said, leaning back against his companion.

Randolf knelt down beside Tom and offered his dagger. "This should do," the Veni Yan priest said.

"Thanks." Tom took the blade and poked at the dry, leathery carcass until he'd made a small hole. Rays of light leaked from the opening.

"I can't watch," Smelly said. He covered his eyes with a clawed hand, but then peeked through his fingers anyway.

The boy made the hole a little larger. Both the Spark around his neck and whatever was hidden inside the squirrel were throbbing together as one.

"Well, I'll be," Percival said, leaning in closer. "What is that?"

"We're about to find out," Tom said as he reached inside the hole.

The tips of his fingers brushed up against something hard in the soft, decaying insides of the dead animal, and he slowly withdrew the glowing object.

It was a small shard of stone, very much like the one that Tom wore around his neck.

"Is that what I think it is?" Abbey asked, eyes wide in wonder.

"A piece of the Spark," Tom said, eyes fixed to the sight.

"Ewww, it's all covered in squirrel guts," Barclay observed, and then started to laugh.

There was a loud thump, and they all looked to see that Stinky had collapsed into the arms of his friend.

"He's very fragile," Smelly said, lowering him to the floor.

Tom ignored the Rats, fascinated by the pulsing stone

in his hand. *This must be why the Dreaming thought the Rat Creatures were important*, he thought.

He rubbed the shard against his leg, removing some of what Barclay had described as squirrel guts, making it glow all the brighter.

"Even when it's covered in muck, I can feel its power," Randolf said.

Tom took hold of the piece around his neck and brought the smaller piece closer, to see if the two would somehow fit together. He felt a sudden pull, and the sliver flew from his hand and attached itself to the larger piece of Spark.

"Wow," Tom managed, when the newly enlarged stone flashed so brightly that the world and his friends suddenly disappeared.

As his eyes cleared of colored spots, Tom found himself in a dark place. The floor was soft and sticky beneath him. At first, he thought he'd somehow been transported to a cave, but then he noticed a low buzzing sound that was growing increasingly louder.

Tom reached down to the fragment of Spark hanging about his neck. The piece was glowing, providing some illumination in the pitch-darkness of the strange chamber.

This vision was different from the others. It was stronger, and more real.

As he raised the Spark and looked around, he realized where the sound was coming from. The light of the Spark shined upon walls made up of multiple golden chambers, and he remembered that he'd seen something similar when he'd gone to market with his parents, only what he'd seen there had been much, much smaller.

He was in a chamber of honeycombs. Really big honeycombs. And the buzzing could only be coming from . . .

The chamber became filled with a swarm of the largest bees he'd ever seen. They were bigger than old Farmer Smith's dog, Euclid, and looked twice as mean.

He'd heard stories of giant bees at market, and how they were found in the southern Valley, and how they were very protective of their honey.

Which probably explained why they were now attacking him.

The bees came at him in a humming cloud, and he turned tail to run. But he came to a screeching stop when he saw that something — three somethings, to be precise — was blocking his way. They were large and furry, and each of them wore a colorful vest — one red, one green, and the other blue.

Bears. Three very large and frightening bears.

They were standing on their hind legs, tossing their heads back with thunderous roars that almost drowned out the buzz of the giant bees.

Almost.

Tom spun away as the bears dropped to all fours and

started charging toward him. Now he was facing the angry swarm of giant bees.

Trapped between bees and bears, with nowhere else to run.

"What the heck is wrong with you?" Percival asked, giving Tom a good shake.

Tom was kneeling on the deck of the *Queen*, the piece of Spark, which was no longer glowing, still in his hand.

"Another vision?" Randolf asked.

Tom's heart was racing as he quickly looked around, half expecting to see the bears and the bees bearing down on him.

"Yes," he said, tucking the piece of Spark back inside his tunic. He tried to sort his jumbled thoughts and figure out what it all meant, the hum of the giant bees and roars of the bears still ringing in his ears.

"So what now?" Percival asked. "Did the vision let you know what's next?"

Tom climbed shakily to his feet. "South," he said. "We're supposed to go south."

"South it is," Percival said with a wink and jogged to the wheelhouse, Abbey and Barclay following close behind.

"Can I help you steer the *Queen*?" Barclay asked.

"I can steer better than you," Abbey proclaimed.

"You can take turns steering, how about that?" Percival

suggested. There was no more arguing, so it must have been fine.

Tom was still shaken from his latest vision and found himself holding on to the ship's railing to steady himself. *What does it all mean?* he wondered. The giant bees and ferocious bears hadn't given him many clues.

He glanced across the deck to see that Randolf and Lorimar were watching him with cautious eyes. Mustering a smile, he waved at them, trying to show the confidence he wasn't exactly feeling at the moment.

Roderick leaped up onto the railing beside him. "Are you okay, Tom?" his best friend in all the world asked.

He wanted to tell Roderick that he wasn't, that he was scared to death, and that the newest visions were the most frightening yet, but he didn't.

He couldn't.

Tom was their leader. They were depending on him — the whole Valley, the world, even — was depending on him.

And most important of all, the Dreaming was depending on him.

"I'm fine," he told Roderick, smiling. "Just a little tired is all." They felt the *Queen of the Sky* bank to the right as the great sky ship began the journey south.

"Being a hero is hard work, isn't it, Tom?" Roderick asked, leaning his head against Tom's shoulder.

"It sure is," Tom answered his friend, gazing out over

the nighttime horizon, fondly remembering a simpler time of picking turnips, when the dreams of being a hero were simply that.

Only dreams.

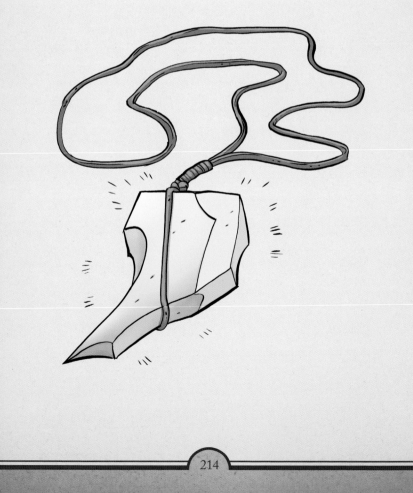

EPILOGUE

Gran'ma Ben was tired of fighting sleep, struggling against the dark force that threatened to pull her down, down, down into the darkness.

She and Prissy had finally left the castle, leaving the fitfully sleeping Queen Thorn's side to venture out into the city.

It had been worse than she'd feared. Wherever they went, they found them: the people of Atheia sound asleep, bound in the grip of nightmare. It didn't take a genius to figure out that something was very wrong with the Dreaming.

They'd tried to find the holy men — the Veni Yan priests — those more attuned to the Dreaming, but even they had succumbed to the threat from beyond. It seemed to strike at the strongest first, those most closely connected to the power of the Dreaming, those who could be a threat.

The weaker it seemed to play with, relishing the fear that it caused. At first, Gran'ma Ben was insulted that it hadn't taken her amongst the first, but she soon came to believe it was a good thing it hadn't. They would try and fight it . . . they would try and get help.

She'd lost Prissy after they decided to leave the city. They were going to find a horse — one that hadn't succumbed to the cursed sleep — and ride out in search of answers, and help.

Gran'ma Ben had been trying to reassure her friend, when she realized she was talking to herself.

Prissy lay in the doorway to the stable, snoring loudly.

She'd tried to wake her up, but there was no use. Prissy was gone, just like all the others.

Just like Thorn.

The weight of her despair had nearly overwhelmed her, but Gran'ma Ben fought through it. Something horrible was happening in the Kingdom, and something told her — that awful gitchy feeling — that it wasn't only there. This was a threat to the entire Valley, and it was coming from the Dreaming.

She'd saddled a horse and tried to make it through the main gates, but the horse had fallen asleep mid-gallop, crashing to the street and sending her flying. That was where she lay now, fighting to stay awake, trying not to be pulled down into the inky depths like all the others had.

But she was so tired. She could feel her eyes growing heavier, as if somebody had attached heavy boulders to them, pulling the lids down over her burning eyes.

Maybe if I rest for just a moment, she thought as her eyelids drifted shut, *then I might be strong enough to fight. . . .*

But Gran'ma Ben knew that it was over, and she felt the world drop out from beneath her just as she closed her eyes. She succumbed to the dark force that had stalked her, that reached out from the Dreaming to drag her down.

It laughed at her, this terrible force, a low and throaty sound. It was happy to finally have caught her. She tried to find it as she squinted into the shadow, opening her third eye. She glimpsed it briefly as it spread its ebony wings and reared back on powerful legs, its joyous laughter turning into the most savage roar.

Never had she seen — *sensed* — something so vicious.

Gran'ma Ben struggled once more, but she just wasn't strong enough to fight it. And as she was dragged deeper and deeper into the depths of shadow, she wondered if there was anybody out there who was.